This month's prize:

A FABULOUS SHARP VIEWCAM!

This month, as a special surprise, we're giving away a Sharp ViewCam**, the big-screen camcorder that has revolutionized home videos!

This is the camcorder everyone's talking about! Sharp's new ViewCam has a big 3" full-color viewing screen with 180° swivel action that lets you control everything you record—and watch it at the same time! Features include a remote control (so you can get into the picture yourself), 8 power zoom, full-range auto focus, battery pack, recharger and more!

The next page contains two Entry Coupons (as does every book you received this shipment). Complete and return *all* the entry coupons; **the more times you enter, the better your chances of winning!**

Then keep your fingers crossed, because you'll find out by November 15, 1995 if you're the winner!

Remember: The more times you enter, the better your chances of winning!*

PRIZE SURPRISE
SWEEPSTAKES

OFFICIAL ENTRY COUPON

This entry must be received by: OCTOBER 30, 1995
This month's winner will be notified by: NOVEMBER 15, 1995

YES, I want to win the Sharp ViewCam! Please enter me in the drawing and let me know if I've won!

Name_____

Address _____ Apt. _____

City   State/Prov.   Zip/Postal Code

Account #_____

Return entry with invoice in reply envelope.

© 1995 HARLEQUIN ENTERPRISES LTD.   CVC KAL

PRIZE SURPRISE
SWEEPSTAKES

OFFICIAL ENTRY COUPON

This entry must be received by: OCTOBER 30, 1995
This month's winner will be notified by: NOVEMBER 15, 1995

YES, I want to win the Sharp ViewCam! Please enter me in the drawing and let me know if I've won!

Name_____

Address _____ Apt. _____

City   State/Prov.   Zip/Postal Code

Account #_____

Return entry with invoice in reply envelope.

© 1995 HARLEQUIN ENTERPRISES LTD.   CVC KAL

Dear Reader,

When my editor at Temptation first approached me about writing three interlocking stories for the Bachelor Arms series, my first thought was *roommates!* Fortunately, it didn't take me long to realize that three adult men living in one apartment wasn't going to work. It would be way too crowded for one thing, and how would they carry on their romances if two other guys were always hanging around? Still, the idea wouldn't let go and I began playing that old writer's game, *What if?*

What if the three men had been roommates in the past? And what if something had happened that had changed their lives forever? Ah, now *there* was an idea rife with dramatic possibilities!

Writing *Passion and Scandal* presented new writing challenges for me. In addition to the task of creating an exciting and emotionally satisfying love story for my hero and heroine, I got to devise an intricate twenty-five-year-old mystery for Steve and Willow to solve while they're falling in love. Together, they finally uncover the truth about what really happened that fateful night at the Bachelor Arms. I hope you enjoy the twists and turns along the way to true love.

And do write—I always like to hear what my readers have to say.

Sincerely,

Candace Schuler

BACHELOR
ARMS

Come live and love in L.A. with the tenants of Bachelor Arms

Bachelor Arms is a trendy apartment building with some very colorful tenants. Meet three confirmed bachelors who are determined to stay single, until three very special women turn their lives upside down; college friends who reunite to plan a wedding; a cynical and sexy lawyer; a director who's renowned for his hedonistic life-style, and many more...including one very mysterious and legendary tenant. And while everyone tries to ignore the legend, every once in a while something strange happens....

Each of these fascinating people has a tale of success or failure, love or heartbreak. But their stories don't stay a secret for long in the hallways of Bachelor Arms.

Bachelor Arms is a captivating place, home to an eclectic group of neighbors. All of them have one thing in common, though—the feeling of community that is very much a part of living at Bachelor Arms.

BACHELOR ARMS

THE TENANTS OF BACHELOR ARMS

Ken Amberson: The odd superintendent who knows more than he admits about the legend of Bachelor Arms.

Zeke Blackstone: The Hollywood director and ladies' man once shared 1G with Jack and Ethan in their bachelor days.

Ariel Cameron: This gorgeous model/actress has found happiness with the love of her life—Zeke.

Eddie Cassidy: Local bartender at Flynn's next door. He's looking for his big break as a screenwriter.

Steve Hart: The P.I. has a lot of heart—and a lot of love for new client Willow. But business has to come before pleasure.

Natasha Kuryan: This elderly Russian-born femme fatale was a makeup artist to the stars of yesterday.

Ethan Roberts: Former roommate of Zeke and Jack, this ex-soap star is preparing for his biggest role yet—public office.

Willow Ryan: With Steve's help, she's determined to find her biological father. But the laid-back detective is a definite distraction.

Eric Shannon: The aspiring screenwriter's tragic suicide has affected the lives of so many people at the B.A.

Faith Shannon: A sweet Georgia peach, now married to Jack and attending med school.

Jack Shannon: The cynical reporter always blamed himself for his brother Eric's mysterious death, but he has been redeemed by the love of a good woman.

Theodore "Teddy" Smith: The resident Lothario—any new female in the building puts a sparkle in his eye.

Candace Schuler
PASSION AND SCANDAL

Harlequin Books

TORONTO • NEW YORK • LONDON
AMSTERDAM • PARIS • SYDNEY • HAMBURG
STOCKHOLM • ATHENS • TOKYO • MILAN
MADRID • WARSAW • BUDAPEST • AUCKLAND

ISBN 0-373-25657-4

PASSION AND SCANDAL

Printed in U.S.A.

There are lots of people who deserve my thanks for their help with this book.

Mary Bracho, for translating the Spanish. M. E. Frolich for steering me toward the right place to look for information about getting into school without a birth certificate. To the nice doctor at LifeCode labs who told me more than I could *ever* hope to understand about DNA. To the Minneapolis P.I. who told me how much it would cost if my heroine needed to hire him—and then advised me to add 25% since it was L.A. To Joyce at the Eden Prairie Police Department for getting back to me so quickly regarding the statute of limitations on hit-and-runs. To my brother, Mark, for his up-to-date expert opinion on condoms. To Harlequin Temptation Senior Editor, Birgit Davis-Todd, for being so patient and understanding. And to my husband, Joe, for being the inspiration for all my heroes. (I promised him I'd say that if he took care of dinner so I could finish this book.)

Prologue

Los Angeles, 1970

A FRENZIED SHRIEK pierced the wall of noise created by the blaring rock music inside apartment 1-G, causing the young woman standing closest to the window to tilt her head toward it. "Listen," she ordered her companions, reaching out to touch the arm of the long-haired, leather-clad young man standing next to her. "What was that?"

"What was what?"

"That," she said. "It sounds like someone's screaming."

"Probably just a siren," suggested another of the group, shrugging as he lifted a joint to his lips for a toke.

"Lots of sirens in L.A.," someone else volunteered. "Nothing to get excited about."

"No, it's not a siren. Someone's screaming," the young woman insisted. She whirled away from the loosely formed circle of people, her long red hair whipping around her shoulders, and reached for the stereo turntable. She hit the play arm, sending it skittering across the record album with a loud screech.

Heads turned toward her and disgruntled protests rose—and then died, unspoken, as the unmistakable sound of a hysterical woman tore through the air like a serrated knife.

Everyone in apartment 1-G froze.

The woman's screams went on unabated, the sound rising and falling jaggedly, as if she were desperately gulping in air between each bloodcurdling shriek.

"What the hell?" someone said.

"Who—"

"Will somebody please call a goddamn ambulance!"

The frantic plea came from outside, too, freeing the party-goers from their stunned inertia. Almost as one they turned toward the door of the apartment, pushing and scrambling as they raced outside and down the interior hallway, all of them coming to an abrupt halt as, by twos and threes, they spilled out onto the courtyard of the Bachelor Arms. Lights were coming on all over the building; windows and doors were opening; other tenants were coming out onto their balconies and into the courtyard to see what all the commotion was about as the woman continued to scream.

"Somebody shut her the hell up!" It was Ken Amberson, the building superintendent who spoke, bellowing out orders as he pushed his way through the crowd. "And the rest of you get back. Now! Shut her up, I said!" he ordered again.

"Come now, child. Control yourself," urged a tiny woman with a soft Russian accent. "You are not the one who is hurt." There were a few more words murmured in a soothing tone—some Russian, some English—and then the sound of a sharp slap rang out. The screaming stopped.

"Someone shoulda done that in the first place," Amberson muttered before turning his attention to the young man who knelt, barefoot and shirtless, over the still, spread-eagled body of another young man. Blood was smeared on his hands and bare chest. More blood, thick and black against the pebbled concrete of the courtyard, spread out in a pool beneath the head of the man on the ground.

"What the hell happened here, Blackstone?" Amberson demanded.

Zeke Blackstone didn't even look up. "Did somebody call an ambulance?" he asked quietly.

"I did," answered the girl who had first heard the screams. She was pushing through the crowd gathered around the body as she spoke. "They said not to move him, not to do anything until they got— Oh, my God." Her face went dead white, as if it had suddenly been drained of blood. "It's Eric."

Amberson put his hand on her shoulder and pushed her out of the way. "I asked you what happened, Blackstone," he demanded again.

"I don't think it will matter if we move him," Zeke murmured. His voice was flat and eerily unemotional but his touch was gentle as he stroked the fallen man's shoulder. "I think he's dead." Though they were softly spoken, the words rippled through the courtyard, sending shock waves through the crowd.

"Dead?" Amberson demanded. "He's dead? How?"

"I don't know," Zeke whispered, still staring down at the body of his friend and roommate. He'd been so alive just a few hours ago. They had been standing in the kitchen—him and Zeke and Ethan—talking about the script Eric and his brother Jack had just sold. "I think he must have fallen and hit his head."

"Fallen from where?" Amberson barked.

"I don't know," Zeke said again. He lifted one arm, gesturing overhead toward the tiny wrought-iron balconies overlooking the courtyard from some of the second- and third-story apartments. "Up there."

An exclamation of disbelief came from someone in the crowd and everyone suddenly started talking at once. The plaintive, insistent sound of a siren spiraled through the soft night air, growing louder and louder as it raced toward them on a futile mission of mercy, gradually drowning out the excited babble of voices.

The redheaded girl started to sob softly then, standing by the body with her hands hanging down by her sides and tears streaming down her cheeks, making the soft mewling sounds of a distressed kitten.

Ethan Roberts reached out and touched the sobbing young woman's shoulder, turning her into his arms.

She wrapped her arms around him, burying her face in his shirtfront. "Oh, Eric," she murmured piteously. "Poor Eric. It's all my fault. I'm the one who saw the woman in the mirror."

"Hush," Ethan murmured soothingly as he cradled her against his chest. "Hush, now, baby. It's all right."

He smoothed his hand over her hair, and leaned down, putting his lips to her ear. His voice was low and crooning. "It's going to be all right, baby. Ethan's got you now."

1

THE VIETNAMESE-OWNED French bakery on the street level should more rightly have been a sleazy bar or a pawnshop but everything else was exactly as Willow Ryan had expected it to be. The stairs creaked. The walls were dingy and needed painting. The narrow hallway was lit by a single naked bulb. The gold letters stenciled on the frosted-glass door panel were peeling at the edges. Gingerly, Willow reached out and put her hand on the doorknob, then hesitated and drew back, giving herself one last chance to reconsider the wisdom of what she was about to do.

At the very least, her actions could end up embarrassing someone. At worst, she might be ruining lives.

If she considered it logically and reasonably, things were fine the way they were. If she went away now and did nothing, they would, in all likelihood, remain fine. But for the first time in her life, Willow found herself unable to be either logical or reasonable.

She had to know.

It was as simple—and as complicated—as that.

She had reached a point in her life when *she had to know*.

Willow smoothed her thick, chin-length hair back behind one ear, took a deep breath, and reached for the doorknob. Turning it firmly in her grasp, she pushed the door open and stepped into an office that looked as if it had been furnished to function as a set for a thirties detective movie.

There was an old-fashioned wooden desk, two chairs with cracked, brown leather upholstery and a low rectangular table littered with a stack of telephone books and a large glass ashtray that looked as if it hadn't been emptied in over a week. The scarred desktop held a telephone, a pencil cup with a motley collection of writing implements and emery boards in it, a leather blotter and a fashion magazine opened to the monthly horoscope column. A lone calendar with a scenic view of the Sierra Mountains in springtime hung on the dingy beige wall behind the desk. The smell of stale cigarette smoke and burned coffee permeated the air, mingling with the scent of fresh-baked bread wafting up from the bakery below. The only thing missing was a tart-tongued, gum-chewing, blond secretary in a tight sweater.

And her hard-boiled boss, of course.

Willow eyed the half-open door leading into what she presumed was an inner office. Maybe the missing secretary and her boss were in there, going over the day's appointments or discussing a case or something. "Hello?" she called, raising her voice slightly. "Anybody here?"

There was no answer.

Willow took a step toward the half-open door. "Hello?" she repeated, louder. "Mr. Hart? Are you here?"

The only response was a soft, muffled noise that bore no resemblance to the usual sounds of business in progress. Willow opened her mouth to call again and then hesitated. Maybe they weren't going over the day's appointments. Maybe they were . . .

She glanced down at the plain gold watch on her wrist. "No, surely not," she muttered to herself.

It was only 9:25 in the morning, after all, and, no matter how disreputable looking, this was a place of business, not a scene from the pages of a potboiler detective novel. Besides, her appointment was for 9:30. She'd carefully arranged her day's schedule around it, leaving her afternoon free for meetings with two of her family's biggest Los Angeles customers. Time was money and she didn't like to waste either one of them.

With a determined step, Willow crossed the small reception area and rapped sharply on the half-open door. "Mr. Hart?"

The low snuffling noise continued unabated and Willow's determination wavered a bit. What if he and his secretary were really in there having sex on the desk? If she just barged in it would be humiliating for all three of them. As much as she hated to do it, maybe she should just write the morning off as wasted time and come back later. Or, better yet, find another detective to help her. Preferably, someone who knew that offices were for working.

She had half turned, ready to leave, when she heard what could only be described as a garbled snort. It didn't sound amorous at all. She leaned toward the door, head tilted as she listened intently.

Someone was snoring.

Loudly.

Willow pushed the door all the way open and stepped inside.

It was another set from the *Maltese Falcon*, incongruously dressed with props from *Rocky*. There was another battered wooden desk, twin to the one in the reception area, another couple of worn chairs, a row of gray metal filing cabinets against one wall and a low wooden credenza under the single large window overlooking the street.

There was also a punching bag suspended in one corner, an open gym bag spilling sweaty socks and damp, ratty-looking towels onto the floor, and a pair of boxing gloves sitting in one of the chairs. A personal computer, obviously brand-new, judging by the empty box and packaging materials strewn about, occupied the other chair. The desktop was buried in a jumbled mess of books, crumpled papers, empty Chinese take-out containers, fast-food wrappers and an open pizza box with two slices of pizza left. The smell of burned coffee came from the empty pot on top of the filing cabinet. The snoring came from the man stretched out on his back on the cracked leather sofa.

Willow sidestepped the gym bag, stepped over a pair of size-twelve Reeboks, and turned off the heating el-

ement under the scorched and stinking coffeepot.
Standing at the end of the sofa, she looked down at its
sleeping occupant.

Several inches too long for his makeshift bed, he lay
with one hand flung over his head and the other resting, palm up, on the floor. His bare, bony feet dangled
over one sagging arm of the too-small sofa. His long
legs were encased in faded jeans, torn at one knee, and
there were pizza stains smeared down the front of the
pale blue T-shirt stretched over his wide chest. His sun-
streaked, dark blond hair stuck up in a half-dozen different directions and there was at least two days' worth
of golden stubble covering his tanned jaw—which hung
open, slackly, revealing a glimpse of toothpaste-ad-
perfect teeth. He was snoring rhythmically, each deep
sonorous exhalation causing the chiseled curve of his
lower lip to vibrate.

This was the man she had come to see? This was
Steve Hart, the private investigator who had been so
highly recommended? The ace detective who was going to help her find out what she had to know? Willow
stood there in uncustomary indecision, staring down
at him for another minute or so, debating with herself.

On the one hand, he looked like a California beach
bum. An aging, rather dissolute California beach bum,
at that. The kind of man who was still trying to coast
through life on his golden good looks and a killer physique. On the other hand, he'd found Angie Claiborne's runaway teenage brother three months after
everyone else had given up.

Maybe this wasn't what it looked like, she thought, trying to give him the benefit of the doubt. Maybe he hadn't passed out on the office sofa after a night of carousing. Maybe he'd been up all night working on a tricky case and this was the first chance he'd had to catch a little shut-eye. And she was already *there*, after all, in his office, her morning already invested in the meeting. It would be foolish to waste both time and opportunity simply because of a misleading first impression.

She reached down and jostled his shoulder. "Mr. Hart?"

The rumbling cadence of his snores didn't change.

She tried again, shaking him a bit harder.

He made a snorting noise, sounding very much like a pig at a trough, and shrugged away from her touch.

Recognizing the signs of a heavy sleeper, Willow abandoned the effort to shake him awake. Carefully setting her briefcase on top of the unused computer, she stepped around the desk to the window. With a flick of her wrist, she opened the old-fashioned venetian blinds, letting in a flood of bright morning light.

The man on the sofa drew his arm down over his eyes and kept on snoring.

"All right," Willow murmured to herself. "You force me to take drastic measures."

A quick perusal of the cluttered desk revealed a large, battered, hardcover book entitled *Accounting For Your Small Business*, half-buried under the pizza box. She picked it up, raised the book over her head with both hands and slammed it down on the floor as hard as she could. It landed with a loud crack that ricocheted through the room like gunfire in a shooting gallery.

The man on the sofa bolted upright before the last echo of sound had faded. "What the hell...?" He lifted his hand in front of his eyes in an effort to block the glaring sunlight, and peered in her general direction. "Who's there?"

"I'm sorry I startled you like that, Mr. Hart, but we have a nine-thirty appointment and I—"

"Who the hell are you?" he growled, squinting at her over his upraised hand. All he could see was a vaguely female shape silhouetted against the light from the window. "And what are you doing in my office?"

"My name is Willow Ryan. We have a nine-thirty appointment and I—"

"Oh, yeah, an appointment. Right." He rubbed his hands over his face, as if to wash away the effects of sleep, then squinted up at her again. He was still unable to make out little more than the outline of a woman. She appeared to be above average height, maybe five foot six, with a slender build and dark hair that gleamed in the nimbus of light that surrounded her head. "Close the blinds, will you? I can't see a thing."

"Are you sure you're awake?"

"I'm sitting up, aren't I?" he snapped. "Close the damn blinds."

With a quick frown to let him know she didn't appreciate being barked at, Willow moved to comply, tilting the blinds just enough so that the sun didn't shine directly in his face. "Better?" she asked tightly.

"Yeah, fine. Thanks." He sighed heavily and scrubbed at his face again. "Look, ah . . . Wilma, is it?"

"Willow," she corrected him. "Willow Ryan."

"Well, look, Willow Ryan, I'm not at my best first thing in the morning, so just bear with me, okay? I'm sorry I snarled at you but I don't turn into a human being until I've had my first cup of coffee."

"Then I'm afraid you're going to continue to be less than human." She nodded toward the coffeemaker, her expression not without a certain amount of sympathy. She, too, needed a stiff shot of caffeine to jump-start her in the morning.

He followed her gaze with his own. "Oh, hell, I burned up another pot. That's the third one this year." He rose to his feet as he spoke and dug into the front pocket of his jeans. "Here, take this." He thrust a couple of folded bills toward her. "Run downstairs to Thuy's and get me a large coffee and a raspberry Danish. Get something for yourself, too, while you're at it. You don't look as if a few extra grams of fat a day would hurt you any."

"Coffee? You want me to run downstairs and get you coffee?"

"Oh, for cryin' out loud. Let's not make a federal case out of it, okay? It's just a lousy cup of coffee, not an attack on modern feminist principles." He waggled the money at her impatiently. "Just do it this once, while I get cleaned up," he wheedled. "I promise I'll do it the next time."

Willow doubted there would ever be a next time but she reached out to take the money; it seemed more expedient than standing there arguing with him. "How do you like your coffee?"

"Black with two sugars," he said, his impatient frown disappearing at her easy capitulation. "And thanks." His lips turned up in smile that revealed a deep dimple in one lean, stubbled cheek. "You're a real lifesaver, Willow."

Willow's breath caught in her throat. Sound asleep and snoring he'd been undeniably attractive. Barely awake, all squinty eyed and grumpy, he'd had a certain rough charm. But with his eyes wide open and his dimple flashing he was easily the kind of man who would have no trouble at all if he wanted to coast through life on looks alone.

Angie Claiborne had said he was good-looking. Actually, the exact words she'd used to describe his appearance were *Greek-god gorgeous* but Willow had discounted that as an example of Angie's usual exaggeration where men were concerned. It looked as if she owed Angie an apology when she got back home to Portland. The man was every bit as gorgeous as she'd said—and then some.

A lesser woman might have been bowled over by the rugged charm of his smile and the sparkle in his bright blue eyes but Willow was made of sterner stuff. She swallowed hard and cleared her throat.

"I'll be back with your coffee in ten minutes," she said crisply, her manner all-business despite the warm flutter of feminine awareness that rippled down her spine. She turned away from the splendor of his dimpled smile and headed for the door, then paused, just for a moment, and glanced back at him over her shoulder. "I'll expect you to be ready to get down to business," she said sternly.

"You got it, sweetheart," he said with a jaunty little salute and a Humphrey Bogart imitation. "Ten minutes."

THERE WERE THREE PEOPLE ahead of her at Thuy's bakery so it was closer to fifteen minutes than ten when Willow returned with the coffee and Danish—but Steve Hart still wasn't ready to get down to business. He wasn't even in his office.

With an exasperated sigh, Willow abruptly decided she'd wasted enough time for one day; much as she hated to admit defeat, it was time to cut her losses and move on. Gorgeous or not, Steve Hart wasn't the only private investigator in the city of Los Angeles and, despite what he'd done for Angie Claiborne and her family, he probably wasn't the best one, either. For one thing, the best private investigator in L.A. would have a much nicer office than this—one where a person could set a cup of coffee and a small bag of pastries on the desk without having to move a ton of garbage out of the way first.

"Here, let me clear some of that junk out of the way for you."

Willow jumped at the sound of his voice, startled to realize he'd come into the room and was right behind her. So close behind her that she could smell the fresh scents of menthol shaving cream and deodorant soap. And warm, red-blooded man.

"Hey, careful there. Don't burn yourself." He plucked the cup of coffee out of her hand before it spilled. "Thuy makes it hot enough to melt steel." He took a quick, appreciative sip, then handed it back. "The place isn't usually so messy," he said, turning away from her to gather up some of the crumpled papers and empty food containers from the desk. "But I've had a real busy couple of days and my last secretary quit over a week ago, so—" he picked up the metal trash can by the desk and began cramming the debris into it as he spoke "—things have kind of gone to hell around here. I'm not much of a housekeeper," he added unnecessarily, flashing his dimple in a self-deprecating, aw-shucks grin meant to charm and disarm.

"No, I can see that you aren't," Willow mumbled in a strangled voice.

It wasn't his dimpled rogue's grin that got to her this time—she wasn't even looking at his face—it was his body. He'd taken off his pizza-stained T-shirt to wash up and had apparently forgotten to replace it with a clean one. The white towel he had slung around his neck didn't even begin to do a decent job of covering him.

He was wide through the shoulders and well muscled without being the least bit bulky. His torso narrowed to a flat, washboard belly and practically nonexistent hips. Crinkly blond hair gilded his well-developed pectorals like gold dust on a living statue—Michelangelo's *David* came immediately to mind—before narrowing into a tempting arrow of silky blond hair that disappeared into the waistband of his snug jeans.

"There, that should be good enough for now," Steve said as he set the trash can back on the floor beside the desk.

"Mmm?" Willow mumbled, unable to think of anything more intelligent in the face of so much glorious masculine pulchritude.

"Just let me get this out of your way—" he grabbed the boxing gloves off of the chair by their laces and tossed them on the sofa "—and you can sit down. Go ahead," he urged when she just stood there. "Take a load off. I'm just going to put these away—" he lifted a stack of file folders up off the desk with one beefy hand "—and grab a clean shirt. It'll just take a second and then we can get started. Okay?"

"Okay," Willow echoed weakly, her gaze following him as he moved away from her toward the filing cabinet.

His back was as appealing as his chest, with long smooth muscles that flexed and rippled under his golden skin with every little movement. Fascinated, her mouth all but hanging open, Willow watched the play of his muscles as he unlocked the top file drawer, dropped the folders in and relocked it. When he bent over to pull open the lowest file drawer, her mouth went dry. He had a better butt than Brad Pitt. Better than Mel Gibson. Better, even, than the anonymous male model whose jeans-clad fanny was currently plastered on billboards all over the country.

Willow forced her gaze away from his rear end. Perfect or not, it was undignified and unprofessional and just plain not nice to ogle him. Not to mention blatantly sexist and politically incorrect. She certainly wouldn't like it if he ogled her like that, she assured herself, staunchly ignoring the insidious little voice in her head that suggested she *would* probably like it very much, indeed, politically correct or not.

She looked down at the top of his still-littered desk, seeking something, anything, to focus her attention on besides Steve Hart's gorgeous body. There was an open ledger book in the center of the desk, its neat columns marred by dark smudges and eraser crumbs. Willow's smooth forehead crinkled up in a disapproving frown as she surveyed the mess he'd made of the ledger. Why on earth, she wondered, would anyone in business for himself in this day and age still be doing his books by hand when affordable PCs and great accounting software had been available for years now? Surely the computer sitting on the chair in front of his desk wasn't his *first*?

And then the file drawer slammed shut with a loud bang and Willow automatically turned her head toward the sound. Steve had taken the towel from around his neck, leaving it in a damp heap atop the filing cabinet, and was pulling a clean T-shirt on over his head. There was a delicious ripple of sinewy muscle as he reached up behind him to draw the soft yellow fabric down to his waist. Then, with his back still to her, he unfastened the fly of his button-front jeans, quickly tucked the T-shirt in, and began buttoning up again.

Willow felt her whole body flush with unaccustomed heat. "For heaven's sake," she muttered, appalled at her reaction to his reverse striptease. "Get a grip, girl," she admonished herself sternly. "You're not seeing anything you haven't seen before." *It's just arranged a whole lot better.*

"Excuse me?" Steve turned around, his hands still at the waist of his jeans as he nonchalantly slipped the last metal button into its buttonhole. "Did you say something?"

Willow hurriedly jerked her gaze away from the vicinity of his fly, focusing it on a point just over his left shoulder. "Your coffee's getting cold," she said, holding it out to him as he approached her.

"Thanks." He plucked the insulated foam cup from her fingers and lifted it to his lips for a long sip. "Mmm, that's good coffee," he murmured, closing his eyes briefly to better savor the flavor. "I'm pretty sure Thuy grinds vanilla in with the coffee beans—" he put the cup down on the edge of the desk and reached for the bag of pastries Willow still held clutched in one sweaty palm "—but she says no, and I've never been able to catch her at it." He opened the top of the bag as he spoke and bent his head, taking a deep, appreciative sniff. "Ah, the tempting scents of fat and sugar. There's nothing else like it. Come to Papa," he crooned as he reached into the bag and pulled out a thick golden pastry, glistening with raspberry filling and smeared with creamy white frosting. "You didn't get anything for yourself," he said, frowning when he realized one pastry was all the bag held.

"I've already had breakfast, thank you."

"Hours ago, I'll bet." He gave her a quick assessing look over the pastry in his hand. "You look like an early riser. Up with the sun, right?"

"Well, yes, usually, but—"

"We'll share," he decided magnanimously, and began to tear the Danish in half.

"No, really." Willow reached out and put her hand on his wrist to stop him from mangling the pastry. "That's your breakfast. I don't want . . ."

Her voice trailed off as heat sizzled up her arm, and she stared, mesmerized by the sight of her long pale fingers against the tanned, hair-roughened skin of his thick, sinewy wrist. She couldn't seem to lift her hand away and her fingers moved, seemingly of their own volition, lightly caressing, unconsciously savoring the incredible heat and texture of him. And then the tendons in his wrist twitched once, hard, as he tightened his fingers on the pastry. Willow looked up and met his gaze, head-on.

Neither one of them said a word for a full ten seconds as they stood there, staring at each other, bright blue eyes boring into golden brown. Frissons of heat passed between them, full of fevered imaginings and rampant speculation, intemperate fantasies and delicious, dizzying possibilities.

And then Willow gasped and snatched her hand away.

And Steve made a strangled noise, deep in his throat—like a chicken that'd just been grabbed by the neck—and beat a hasty retreat to the other side of his desk. "Well, let's get down to business, shall we?" He dropped the untouched Danish back into the bag and set it aside. Sitting down behind the desk, he reached for a stack of papers, busily flipping through them as if he were trying to find something important. "I suppose the agency has already filled you in on the basics?"

"Agency?" Willow croaked. She cleared her voice and tried again. "What agency?" Angie hadn't said anything about going through any agency; she'd just given Willow a phone number and said to call it.

"Did they tell you I require someone who can type at least eighty words a minute? And who can take dictation?" he added, making up the requirements as he went along. "You can take dictation, can't you?" he asked, hoping she couldn't.

He didn't want another secretary who looked at him as if she'd like to eat him up with a spoon, even when— no, *especially* when—he was so strongly tempted to

return the favor. His last secretary had walked out—
well, stormed out, actually—when he'd finally convinced her that his warm regard and affection for her
as an employee would never translate into anything
more. He'd hated like hell to have to hurt her feelings;
she'd been a real sweet girl and a damned good secretary. Or so he'd thought, until he discovered the un-
holy mess she'd made of his bookkeeping system before
she left, which hadn't been all that good to begin with.

"I'll expect you to make the coffee every morning,"
he said, determined to avoid another fiasco like the last
one. "Or to run down to Thuy's if the pot's on the blink.
I'll also want you to drop my laundry and cleaning off
every week at By George down the block. And walk my
dog and, ah . . . You're shaking your head," he noted,
relieved. "Does that mean you don't want the job?"

"Yes. It means I don't want the job," Willow said. "It
means I—"

"Great. Then how would you like to have—"

"—didn't come here for a job in the first place," Willow finished.

"—lunch with me today?" Steve said at the same
time.

They stared at each other over the desk, both of them
suddenly realizing they didn't have the faintest idea of
what the other was talking about. Steve managed to
gather his thoughts together first.

"We seem to have gotten our wires crossed somewhere," he said, the expression in his blue eyes sharp
and considering as he stared at her. She was wearing an

elegant charcoal gray pin-striped suit and a softly tailored white silk blouse. Her small hoop earrings and the
heavy serpentine chain around her neck were real gold.
Her dark brown hair was cut in a sleek, sophisticated
style that swooped down from an off-center part, emphasizing her large golden brown eyes and delicately
chiseled jaw. The black leather briefcase she'd placed
on top of his computer would have cost four hundred
dollars on Rodeo Drive. The woman was definitely
upper-management material. "Obviously, you're not
from the employment agency."

Willow shook her head. "No."

"And you don't want a job as my secretary."

"No."

"I see. So . . ." There was no idle sexual speculation
in his eyes now; his gaze was direct and focused, intent
on the possibility of a case. "What do you want, Willow Ryan?"

She met his direct look with one of her own. "I want
you to help me find my father."

2

IT WASN'T A REQUEST Steve heard every day but it wasn't one he'd never heard before, either. Teenagers weren't the only ones who ran away from home when life got to be too much. "Why don't you sit down," he said kindly, gesturing at the chair behind her, "and tell me about it."

Willow nodded and sat, nervously perching herself on the edge of the chair. "I got your name from Angie Claiborne," she explained. "She said you found her younger brother, Teddy, when no one else could. That even with practically no clues and nothing to go on, you didn't give up until you'd brought him home to his family."

Steve nodded, waiting for her to go on, knowing she'd get to it in her own time. Lots of clients had to talk around the real reason they'd come to him before they got down to it.

"I remember Teddy," he said. "Skinny kid with a wild mop of black hair. Tall for his age. Big, scared eyes." Teddy Claiborne had been one of the good cases. One of the satisfying ones, where he'd been able to get to the kid before he'd been completely lost to the streets. It didn't always work out that way. "How is Teddy?"

"He's doing much better. He's back in school and doing okay. Angie says the whole family's in therapy."

"Glad to hear it," Steve said, and meant it. It was good to know an effort was being made to correct the circumstances that had sent the kid running in the first place.

Willow smoothed her hands down her skirt. "Angie said to tell you hello," she said.

"Next time you see her, tell her I said hello back," he said easily, still patiently waiting for her to get to the point.

She bit her lip, wondering where to start.

"It's usually easiest just to jump in and tell it," Steve prompted.

"I don't have a lot of information to give you," she warned him.

"Let's just start with the information you do have, and see where it goes. How long has your father been missing?"

"Twenty-five years."

"Twenty-five . . . You're looking for your biological father, then? You're adopted?"

"I'm looking for my biological father but, no, I'm not adopted. Not officially. I was raised by my aunt and uncle. Mostly, anyway." One corner of her mouth lifted in a little half smile. "It's a little complicated to explain."

"It usually is, but try."

"Yes, well..." Willow smoothed her skirt down over her thighs, taking a moment to gather her thoughts. "I grew up in a commune."

"A commune? You mean with hippies? Back to nature? Turn on and drop out? That kind of commune?"

Willow nodded, sending a heavy sheaf of shiny brown hair swinging down over her cheek. She hooked it behind her ear with the tip of one well-manicured finger. "Pretty much, although it was more back to nature than drug oriented, even in the very beginning. My aunt Sharon and her husband Dan, and about fifteen others, founded it in the mid-sixties. It was just a farm, really, located outside Bend, Oregon, in the Cascade Mountains, but Dan—he was a third-year law student before he dropped out—made sure it was legally incorporated as a real township. Unlike most communes of that era, they've managed to survive, more or less intact, right on into the nineties. Are you familiar with Blackberry Meadows' Pure Fruit Essences?"

Steve accepted the apparent change of subject without blinking. "Organically grown, pesticide-free, sugar-free jams and jellies? Available in limited quantities at the toniest gourmet shops and health food stores in town? That Blackberry Meadows?"

"That's us. The commune, I mean."

"Raspberry Rhapsody is my favorite," Steve informed her. "I put it on my frozen toaster waffles. It makes a good ice-cream topping, too."

"I'll be sure to tell Sharon that," Willow said, smiling a little when she thought of what her aunt's reaction would be to having her healthful fruit spreads used as a topping for junk food. "According to family legend, she cooked up the very first experimental batch of Blackberry Bliss Pure Fruit Essence on an old woodburning stove. It was so good, she ended up practically denuding the farm's blackberry patch to make enough to sell to a couple of the local merchants. Hard cash wasn't easy to come by back then," she confided, "so everyone did what they could. Today, we make six different flavors and sell it in select markets up and down the West Coast."

Steve nodded and waited for her to go on.

"So, anyway..." She smoothed her hands down the front of her skirt again, suddenly not at all anxious to get to the heart of the matter. She was desperately afraid he would say he couldn't help her, that there wasn't enough information to go on.

"I was born on February 26, 1971," she said. "My mother left Blackberry Meadows when I was three months old, in April of that year, leaving me with Sharon and Dan. Two months after she left, she was hit by a car while crossing Hollywood Boulevard." Willow recited the facts calmly, as if they had long ago lost the power to hurt her, but her hands were rubbing up and down the tops of her thighs as she spoke. "Sharon didn't even know my mother was dead until almost a month after it happened."

"And your father?" Steve asked gently.

"I don't know who he is. Nobody knows."

"Is that what it says on your birth certificate? Father unknown?"

Her hesitation was slight but telling, clearly telegraphing her uneasiness with the subject. Her hands stilled on her lap, pressing down against the tops of her thighs, as if she were trying to keep herself from jumping up and running away from his questions. "I don't have a birth certificate."

Only his quick reading of her distress enabled him to hide his astonishment. "No birth certificate?" he asked mildly. "How did that happen?"

"I was born at home," she explained, "in a log house, with Sharon and a couple of the other women serving as midwives. Back then, the inhabitants of Blackberry Meadows considered birth certificates to be a meaningless establishment convention, just like marriage licenses."

"How were you able to register for school? Or get a social security card? Or a driver's license?"

"Sharon used the family Bible as proof of when and where I'd been born. She recorded all the births in the commune that way. Marriages, too. It's unorthodox but perfectly legal. After that, it was just a matter of taking the school's aptitude tests and placement exams to figure out which grade to put me in."

"I take it they didn't start you in kindergarten like everyone else?"

"No," she said. "I was home schooled until I was eleven. There were three ex-teachers in the family, so it wasn't nearly as unconventional as it sounds," she added defensively. "I scored two grade levels above my age group on the placement exams and attended regular schools from then on. I have a Bachelor's degree in Accounting and an M.B.A. and, as soon as I graduated, I took over the management of the family business and—" She stopped abruptly, realizing she was rambling like an idiot in an attempt to balance the unconventionality of her early childhood with her very conventional life since then.

But none of what she'd just told him was going to help him find her father. It was time to give him the pitifully few clues she did have and pray they would be enough.

"My mother wrote to Sharon twice while she was living in Los Angeles," she said, reaching for the briefcase she'd set on top of the computer. She laid it on her lap and unsnapped the locks. "She was working as a waitress while she tried to break into acting. In April of 1970, she wrote that she'd gotten a small part in a soap opera and that she was moving to a new apartment with a girlfriend. Soon after, there was another letter saying she'd met a really great guy and that the writers on the soap opera had made her part on the show a continuing one. It sounded as if everything was really going her way, that she might actually make it as an actress. And then, after that, nothing until September when she showed up at Blackberry Meadows, sick, broke and four months pregnant."

"Alone, I assume."

"Yes."

"And she never said another word about this supposedly great guy who'd apparently gotten her pregnant, then abandoned her?" he said, unable to hide his
contempt for a man who would do such a thing. "Not
even to her sister?"

"Not a word."

"Are you sure you want to find this character?" Steve
asked, already knowing what she'd say. She wouldn't
have come to him if she hadn't already made up her
mind. Still, he felt obligated to point out a few home
truths. "If by some wild chance I do manage to locate
him for you—and, believe me, with the information
you've given me so far, the chances are slim to none. But
if I *do* locate him, he might very well refuse to see you
or to acknowledge you in any way. Have you thought
of that? How you'll feel if that happens?"

"Yes, I've thought of that. But I still want to try." Her
hands curled into fists on her lap. "I *have* to try."

"All right," Steve said, acquiescing without an argument; he knew grim determination when he saw it.
"Let's see the letters."

Willow opened her briefcase, withdrew a small
manila envelope and handed it to him across the desk.
"There are some pictures in there, too, and a card,
written to my mother and signed with the initial *E*," she
said, watching as he opened the envelope and tipped
the contents out on top of the ledger on his desk. "The
three Polaroids are of my mother and me, but the others are from her time in L.A."

"No envelopes?" Steve asked, as he picked up one of the letters and unfolded it.

"No, Sharon just saved the letters," Willow said, apologizing for her aunt's oversight. She snapped the locks on the briefcase closed and set it on the floor by her chair. "She had no way of knowing, back then, that the envelopes might be important someday."

The two letters were short, overflowing with the enthusiasm and emotion of youth, woefully inadequate when it came to hard facts. "'I finally got a part!'" Steve read out loud as he scanned the letters. "'I play a nurse at Meadowland General on "As Time Goes By."'...I met this really great guy.... Christine and I move into our new apartment next week.... The writers expanded my role and made the nurse a continuing character. Maybe now I'll be able to cut down on my hours at the restaurant!'" Both letters were signed "Love, Donna" and both were written in purple ink on the kind of standard pink writing paper that could still be found in any stationery or office supply store. Steve set them aside and picked up the card.

The envelope had neither stamp nor address, suggesting that it had been hand delivered. Steve lifted the tucked-in flap and extracted the card. It was one of those romantic soft-focus ones with a picture of a hand-holding couple walking on a sunset beach. Someone had written *you* and *me* over the couple, with arrows pointing down so there would be no mistake about which was which. Inside was a sappy Rod McKuen verse about the nature of love and the inked-in sentiment, "You really blew my mind last night, babe. Love, E."

Steve set it on top of the other two letters and picked up the pictures. The first two showed Willow and her mother, obviously only minutes after the delivery. The newborn baby was red and squalling; the mother looked exhausted, her expression a touching mixture of triumph and sadness. The third snapshot showed mother and child a few weeks later. The baby was plump, healthy and content, tenderly cradled in her mother's arms. The mother appeared marginally less exhausted but the sadness hadn't left her eyes. If anything, it seemed to have grown, overshadowing her obvious pride in her baby girl.

"The other five snapshots are from when she lived in Los Angeles before I was born," Willow said as Steve laid the pictures of mother and child on top of the letters.

For a second, Steve thought he was looking at a completely different woman. The Donna Ryan in these pictures was as different from the Donna Ryan in the previous ones as a rosebud was from a dried flower. Even the outlandish fashions of the early seventies couldn't obscure her fresh, innocent beauty. She was an enchanting young temptress with huge, luminous eyes set at a slant above high, chiseled cheekbones. A waterfall of straight, gleaming mahogany red hair flowed down her back, hanging nearly to the hem of her psychedelic tie-dyed minidress. She stood alone in front of a wrought-iron gate, her delicately voluptuous body in profile to the camera, her head turned to face the photographer. She was smiling—a happy, seductive smile meant for whomever was taking the picture.

Steve glanced up at Willow, studying her for a moment over the top of the desk. "You have her eyes," he said, and he set the picture aside.

Willow said nothing, watching him while he studied the other photographs. They were all group shots, various combinations of Willow's mother with another young woman and four equally young men. They appeared to have been taken at the same location as the first one, at the same time, as if the camera had been passed around among the group so they could take pictures of each other.

"I suppose you're thinking that one of these guys might be your father," Steve said.

It wasn't a question but Willow answered it anyway. "I think it's possible. Maybe. She must have kept the pictures for a reason. They were the only things, besides the card and a few clothes, that she brought with her when she came to Blackberry Meadows."

Steve nodded vaguely and went back to studying the photographs. Something about the building in the background seemed familiar. Maybe it was the predominantly Spanish architecture that made him think he'd seen it before, but he didn't think so. Faded pink stucco walls and fanciful wrought-iron balconies were common in many of the old neighborhoods in and around Los Angeles but the vaguely Moorish tower jutting up on one side of the building was unique. He opened a desk drawer, rooting around until he found a magnifying glass. Fanning the photographs out, he studied each one more closely, scrutinizing every detail.

He knew the building, all right.

He also recognized two of the faces.

"What?" Willow demanded, unable to bear the suspense a moment longer. "What is it?"

Steve took one more long look, just to be sure. "This building—" he tapped one of the photographs with the edge of the magnifying glass "—is the Bachelor Arms apartments. It's only a few miles from here."

"And?" She knew there was an *and;* she could see it in his face.

"And one of the guys in these pictures is Zeke Blackstone."

Willow's mouth dropped open in astonishment. "Zeke Blackstone?" she echoed. "The *actor?* Are you sure?"

"Take a good look at the guy on the far left." He extended both picture and magnifying glass across the desk. "If it isn't Blackstone, it's his twin brother."

"My God. I think you're right," she said, looking past the long hair and the tight bell-bottom jeans with the peace sign sewn on the knee. "I think it *is* Zeke Blackstone."

"Now take a look at the guy standing next to him, the one with his arm around your mother."

Willow looked as ordered, her forehead crinkling up as she peered through the magnifying glass. He had long sideburns and a thick, drooping mustache. "Is he an actor, too?"

"He used to be, years ago. Don't you recognize him?"

Willow shook her head. "Who is he?"

"That's Ethan Roberts. If the Republicans have their way in the next election, he'll be Senator Roberts."

Willow's golden brown eyes widened until they threatened to fill up her whole face. "Oh, my God," she murmured. Ethan Roberts. The single initial *E* on the card to her mother. And there he was in the picture, with his arm slung casually around Donna's shoulders. After all these years of wondering, was it really going to be that easy? She stared across the desk at Steve. "Do you really think it might be him?" she whispered.

"It might," he said, emphasizing the second word. "*Might,*" he repeated when she continued to sit there with the picture and magnifying glass clasped in her hands, staring at him with a look of shimmering hope in her eyes. "Or it might not." He brushed aside a pile of papers and reached for the telephone. "There's only one way to find out."

"You're going to call him? Right now? Right this very minute?" The last few words rose to a high-pitched squeak as her voice tightened with panic and excitement. She closed her eyes and took a deep breath to calm herself. "Do you think that's the best way to handle it?"

"You want to know, don't you?"

"Well, yes, but ... I mean—" She lifted her hands, realized she still held the photograph and magnifying glass, and put them down on the desk, all without shifting her gaze from his. "You can't just call and ask him if...if..." She floundered, unable to think of a way to phrase the question. "How *do* you ask a man if there's any chance he could be your father?" she wondered out loud.

"You just ask," Steve said, as if it were the simplest thing in the world. "But don't worry, I'm not going to do it over the phone." He punched in a three-digit number. "Right now, all I'm going to do is call and set up an appointment to see him. Yes," he said into the receiver. "Do you have a residential listing for Ethan Roberts?" There was a moment of silence while the operator checked. "How about a number for his campaign headquarters? That must be listed." He listened for a moment, then pressed the disconnect button and redialed.

Willow sat in tense silence, her nerves stretched tight, her hands clutched together in her lap, listening as Steve was transferred up the chain of command at Ethan Roberts' campaign headquarters until, finally, he reached someone with the authority to take a message.

"No, I'm sorry, I can't discuss the matter with anyone but Mr. Roberts," he said to the person on the other end of the phone. "Yes, I realize you're his campaign manager but, as I said to the two people I talked to before you, it's a private matter. Highly sensitive and confidential. If you'll just tell him it concerns a young woman named Donna Ryan—" He spelled out the last name. "Yes, that's right. Donna Ryan. Her daughter has some questions she hopes Mr. Roberts can answer. He can reach me at the number I gave you anytime, day or night."

"Now what?" Willow asked when he put the receiver down.

"Now, we wait."

"How long?"

"Hard to tell. Maybe a few minutes. A few hours. Maybe a few days. It depends on how quickly his campaign manager gets the message to him. And how urgent he thinks it is."

"A few *days?*" she wailed. "I don't think I can stand the suspense for that long."

"You've stood it for twenty-four years. Another few days shouldn't make any difference."

"I know, but to be this close and—"

The phone rang, making them both jump.

"Do you think it's him?" Willow whispered. "Already?"

Steve smiled, looking like a shark who'd just scented blood in the water. "Only one way to find out." He picked up the receiver. "Steve Hart," he said.

"This is the Ethan Roberts for U.S. Senate campaign office," chirped a disembodied female voice. "I'm calling in regard to a message you left for Mr. Roberts concerning a Ms. Donna Ryan."

"Yes." Steve punched the speaker button so Willow could listen in. "Go ahead."

"Mr. Roberts has asked me to inform you that he will
be in San Francisco until very late this evening attending a fund-raising benefit at the Mark Hopkins Hotel.
He regrets that he cannot address the matter of Ms.
Ryan immediately but asks if it would be convenient for
you to meet with him at his home tomorrow morning
at 9:00 a.m., at which time he'll be glad to offer whatever help or information he can."

"Tomorrow morning would be fine."

"Very good," the woman said, and rattled off the
address. "Mr. Roberts will be expecting you for breakfast."

The line went dead, filling the room with the buzz of
a disconnected telephone. Steve pushed the speaker
button and the buzzing stopped.

"Oh, my God," Willow said softly and reached out,
grabbing the edge of the wooden desk for support. Her
face was dead white.

"Jesus, you're not going to faint, are you?"

"I don't . . . know," she whispered, and swayed forward in her chair.

Steve jumped up and came swiftly around the desk.
"Put your head down between your knees," he ordered, cupping the back of her head to make her do it.

"I'm all right. Really. I never faint." She resisted the
downward pressure of his hand, turning her head to
look up at him instead. "It's just so..." She took a deep
trembling breath, as if to steady herself, and then sank
forward, like a slowly deflating balloon, and pressed
her forehead against his stomach. "I didn't think it

would hit me this hard," she confessed, whispering the words into the soft fabric of his yellow T-shirt.

Steve went stock-still, his whole body tightening under a sudden barrage of conflicting emotions. The weight of her head pressed against the taut muscles just north of his waistband, the silkiness of her heavy hair sliding through his fingers, the smell of her perfume at such close range, aroused every aggressive masculine instinct he possessed. The soft shaking of her shoulders, the trembling sound of her breathing as she tried to control herself, had him struggling for tenderness.

It wasn't as if he'd never had a woman turn to him for comfort before. In his line of work, knowing how to comfort a distraught woman—or a man or child, for that matter—was as important as knowing what questions to ask and where to look for the answers. But if anyone had told him, even ten minutes ago, that he'd be standing in his office with a beautiful woman's face practically pressed into his groin, trying to think of ways to comfort her instead of get her on the sofa, he would have laughed and said they were crazy.

And yet, here he was, stroking her hair and hoping like hell she didn't notice the part of him that had suddenly sprung to rigid attention beneath his jeans.

"It's okay now, honey," he murmured soothingly. "Just take a couple of deep breaths and you'll be all right. No sense getting upset until we know if he's the right one, now, is there?"

Willow sniffled and shook her head. "No, you're right." She put her hand on his waist, pushing a little away from him, and tilted her head back. "I'm sorry," she said, gazing up at him with eyes that glimmered with unshed tears. She tried to smile, her lips quirking up at the corners in a self-deprecating, embarrassed little grimace devoid of any real humor. "I'm acting like a crazy person."

"I guess you're probably entitled to act a little crazy," he murmured gruffly, gazing down at her as he mindlessly smoothed his palm over the back of her head. "It's not every day you find out you might be related to the next senator from California." He grinned, revealing the dimple in his lean cheek. "The fact that he's a Republican was bound to make the shock worse."

She smiled for real, as he had meant her to, honest amusement replacing some of the dazed confusion in her slanted golden brown eyes. Steve lifted his free hand, intending to brush back the lock of hair that had fallen over her face. Somehow, he found his hand cupping her cheek, instead, and he extended his thumb, slowly brushing it across her lower lip.

She gasped once, a tiny breath of sound, and went very still in his hands, like a small, fragile animal instinctively freezing to avoid detection by something bigger and infinitely more dangerous than she was.

He stroked her lip again, and the curve of her cheek, and the line of her delicately chiseled jaw, fascinated by the shape and texture beneath his caressing thumb. She was soft everywhere. Soft lips. Soft skin. Soft hair, as dark and thick as his mother's mink coat, as shiny as the satin ribbons his younger sister used to wear in her hair when she was a little girl.

He had a sudden, searing vision of laying Willow Ryan down, naked, on that mink coat, her soft pale skin gleaming like a pearl against the lush fur. He imagined tying her up with the satin ribbons, winding the long shiny strands around her ankles and thighs and wrists, around her arms and waist and breasts, tying it all up with a pretty bow beneath her chin. And then slowly untying it all again, revealing her softness inch by delicious inch, like a present meant just for him.

And he could do it, he thought. He could have her right here, right now. She was vulnerable and off-balance, looking to him to solve her problems for her. It would be so easy. With just a little persuasion, he could have her lying naked beneath him on the old leather couch against the wall. One kiss, two, and she would be his. He tightened his hand on the back of her head, drawing her up out of the chair. Willow rose to his touch like a marionette in the hands of the puppet master.

He touched his lips to hers once . . . twice . . . three times . . . soft, sweet, coaxing little baby kisses that had her parting her lips in anticipation of more. He gave it to her, caressing her lips with his in a moist openmouthed kiss. She made a small yearning sound, deep in her throat, a tiny whimper of uncertain resistance and arousal, barely loud enough to be heard.

It was enough to jolt Steve out of the the sensual fog that enveloped him. Good God! What was he think-

ing? What was he *doing*? He didn't get sexually involved with clients. It was his one unshakable,
irrevocable rule.

She'd come to him needing help. Trusting. Vulnerable. And, then, when her defenses were at their lowest, when she'd turned to him in a moment of need,
seeking the simple comfort of a human touch, he'd
gotten a hard-on and started daydreaming about rav-
ishing her on the office furniture! There were names for
men who preyed on the vulnerabilities of women but
they were ones that had never been—and never would
be!—applied to him.

Deliberately, Steve relaxed his hands, releasing her
head, and stepped back. "Feel better now, sweetheart?" he asked, playing Bogart once more. Trying to
keep it light. Trying to reassure her.

"Ah . . . yes," she said and, amazingly, she was. His
gentle kiss had been exactly what she needed to chase
away the sick, confused feeling in her stomach. "Yes, I
am."

"Well, then, since we aren't going to be able to talk
to Roberts until tomorrow," he said casually, as if they
both weren't breathing just a little too fast, "how 'bout
we take a ride over to the Bachelor Arms? It'll give you
a chance to look at the place you were probably con-
ceived."

3

WILLOW TIPPED HER HEAD back against the white leather upholstery of Steve Hart's 1967 baby blue Mustang convertible and let the Los Angeles sun beat down on her face. She'd suggested driving her car to the Bachelor Arms, since it was parked just two doors down from Thuy's bakery, but Steve had taken one look at the sedate gray sedan she'd rented from Hertz and walked right on by it. They'd had to walk three blocks to the secured parking lot where he kept his car—which qualified as a major hike to most Californians, who drove everywhere. But now, sitting in the sporty little convertible with the sun beating down on her closed eyelids and the wind dancing in her hair, Willow decided the blister forming on her left heel was worth it.

It was one of those perfect Southern California days. The kind of day that made millions of people decide Los Angeles was the only place they wanted to live despite earthquakes, urban crime and high taxes. Willow stretched a little, pushing her shoulders back against the soft leather seat, and sighed in contentment, indulging herself with imagining they were driving along the Coast Highway, heading north, with the land rising up, rich and golden, on one side of them and the Pacific crashing against the beach on the other.

And then there was the squeal of brakes. A horn honked in response. And someone shouted an anatomically impossible obscenity.

Willow's lovely fantasy vanished into thin air. She sighed and opened her eyes—just as they passed a billboard advertising the low, low, incredibly low interest rates available at a certain friendly neighborhood bank.

She straightened in the soft bucket seat, automatically smoothing her skirt down over her knees. "It just occurred to me that we haven't discussed your fee," she said, raising her voice to be heard above the sound of Jan and Dean singing about a little old lady from Pasadena and her lead foot.

Steve reached over and turned the radio down a notch. "Excuse me?"

"Your fee," Willow said, appalled she had forgotten about it until now. She'd been distracted, certainly, but it wasn't like her to neglect to get the financial aspects of any deal settled first.

Steve gave her a considering glance out of the corner of his eye as he downshifted into first to take the corner at Santa Monica and Westwood. "Seventy-five dollars an hour with a six-hundred-dollar nonrefundable retainer up front," he said, quoting his highest rates. He charged most of his cases a lot less than that. Many were done pro bono. But a woman in a seven-hundred-dollar suit and real gold jewelry could afford to pay top price. "Plus expenses."

Willow was prepared to pay whatever it took to find her father, of course, but— "Seventy-five dollars an hour?" she said skeptically, automatically haggling for a better deal. "Isn't that a little high, even by L.A. standards?"

"Naw, those are my discounted rates. Just for you, sweetheart," he said with his Bogie imitation. He slanted her a lazy glance as he changed lanes to pass an in-line skater who was making illegal use of the roadway. "If they're too high maybe we can take it out in trade."

A warm little flutter of awareness slid down her spine; twin to the feeling that had rippled through her the first time he'd flashed his dimple; distant cousin to what she had felt when he kissed her. It was a dangerous feeling, and inappropriate, given the circumstances. "And just what exactly do you mean by that?" she asked, giving him a sharp look from under lowered brows.

"Not what you're thinking," he chided her, lying through his perfect teeth. Because she was right, it was *exactly* what she was thinking. Not for real, of course. He wouldn't sink so low as to suggest she trade sexual favors for his services as an investigator. But a man could dream, couldn't he?

And he'd been dreaming, all right, his fingers closing tighter and tighter on the leather-wrapped steering wheel as he'd darted glances at her out of the corner of his eye. She'd sat there with her face turned up to the sun like a pleasure-seeking sybarite, her breasts pushing against the front of her tailored silk blouse and her sleek gray pin-striped skirt sliding higher up her thighs every time she squirmed against the leather. God, he wished she weren't a client!

"What I had in mind," he said, "was a simple exchange of professional services."

Willow considered that for a moment. "You mean barter?" she asked innocently, as if the concept were unfamiliar to her. During her early years on the commune, before she'd taken over the management of Blackberry Meadows' Pure Fruit Essences and made them all rich beyond their wildest dreams, barter had been the primary means of economic survival. Willow had been better at it than anybody.

"I guess we could work something out." She shifted in her seat, crossing her legs as she angled her body toward him, and hooked a sheaf of flyaway hair behind her ear. "What did you have in mind?"

Was she doing that on purpose? he wondered. Using her sex appeal to try to distract him? He slanted another glance at her out of the corner of his eye. As far as he could tell she had nothing but business on her mind. The sexiness was just a natural part of her, an inborn quality that even her I'm-a-highly-skilled-professional-woman outfit couldn't hide.

"Did all those fancy degrees you've got teach you anything about computers?" he asked.

"The one you had in your office had a 386SX processor, with 4 megabytes of memory, a 150-meg disk drive and a 300-dpi laser printer," she said, showing off.

Making what you had to offer as attractive as possible was the first step to successful bartering. "You should have gotten a Pentium processor with 12 megabytes of memory, a gigabyte of disk space and a built-in CD-ROM. It has a lot more power for not a lot more money. And a 600-dpi printer would give you much better quality graphics."

"I don't want better quality graphics," he grumbled, turning his attention back to the traffic as it slowed for a construction crew. "I just want to computerize my accounting system."

"Well . . ." Now that she knew what he wanted, she could settle into some serious haggling. "Judging by the ledger I saw on your desk, I'd say you don't even have a decent manual system at the moment. It'd probably take me, oh . . . two or three days just to make sense of the mess you made of it, then, say, another day to get a new system set up. So, four days total should do it." She nonchalantly plucked a nonexistent piece of lint off her skirt and held it out over the car door for the wind to take. "I make nearly four thousand dollars in that time with Blackberry Meadows," she said, rounding to the nearest hundred. "Of course," she added, setting him up for the kill, "if I have to teach you to use the computer first, we should probably add another week to that estimate."

"Is that four thousand a week before or after taxes?"

"Before," she admitted. "But I don't think that's relevant. Your seventy-five dollars an hour is a before-tax figure, too."

The lady was one sharp cookie. A sharp, *sexy* cookie, whether she was trying to be or not. He'd never realized a business discussion could be so damned stimulating.

"Do we have a deal?" she asked.

"I'm thinking." He stalled, just to make her work for it.

"I'd be willing to throw in two of those days of training for free as a gesture of goodwill."

"Deal," he said, and downshifted into another turn.

They both smiled, each satisfied that they had made the better bargain.

THE BACHELOR ARMS was located on Wilshire Boulevard between a small Italian grocery store and a brick-fronted bar named Flynn's. It was an aging grande dame of a building, a great lady from a bygone era with sun-washed pink stucco walls, wrought-iron balconies, graceful arched windows and a fanciful turret rising up from one corner of the slanting red-tiled roof. Originally constructed in the twenties by a successful real-estate speculator, it had undergone several incarnations over the years, suffering the ignominious fate of having its spacious, high-ceilinged rooms chopped into ever smaller apartments. But somehow, through all the changes it had endured, it never lost its original elegance and glamour.

Willow stared at it, her gaze darting back and forth between the building and the photographs she held in her hands. The banana tree in front was taller now than it was in the pictures and there were some lush flower beds that hadn't been planted back in 1970, but it was plain to see how Steve had so easily recognized it. It had hardly changed at all in the last twenty-five years.

"Are you going to sit in the car all day and stare at it?" Steve asked, looking down at her from where he stood on the sidewalk. "Or are you going to get out and come in with me?"

Willow looked up, startled to realize he was standing on the other side of the door, holding it open for her. "Oh. Sorry." She slipped the photographs into the pocket of her suit jacket and swung her legs out of the car.

Steve permitted himself a quick glance before looking away; he couldn't really be blamed for picturing her ankles with satin ribbons wrapped around them. That was just the kind of fantasy that stuck in a man's mind.

"Why don't we put that in the trunk?" he said, when she leaned over and reached into the back seat of the open convertible for her briefcase. "You're not going to need it here and there's no sense lugging it around."

Willow handed it to him without comment, waiting on the sidewalk as he walked around behind the car. He stowed the briefcase and then, to her secret amusement, leaned over and carefully buffed off the fingerprints he'd left on the gleaming paint job with the sleeve of his navy sport jacket.

"She's a classic," he said when he looked up and caught her smiling. "And classics deserve to be pampered."

"I'm surprised you park her in the street if you feel that way."

"This is a pretty good neighborhood," he said, taking her elbow to escort her up the brick path to the front steps of the building. His dimple flashed briefly. "And she's got an alarm that'll wake the dead if anyone so much as breathes on her too hard."

The front door of the Bachelor Arms had a keyed security lock, meant to keep everyone but tenants out of the building. There was a small brass panel set into the pink stucco wall on one side of the door. It held a column of push-button doorbells, each neatly labeled with a name and apartment number. Above it was a gleaming brass plaque, about two feet square, with the name of the building deeply engraved in bold Gothic script. Below it someone had scratched the words *Believe the legend*.

"What do you suppose that means?" Willow asked as Steve reached out to press the buzzer marked Manager. "What legend?"

"I have no idea. Probably just some juvenile delinquent's idea of a joke."

"It is referring to the legend of the lady in the mirror," said a soft voice from behind them. The accent was faintly Russian.

Steve and Willow turned as one. A tiny woman, not much more than five feet tall, was standing at the bottom of the wide brick steps. She was dressed in a hot pink jogging suit and high-top sneakers. A silver lamé baseball cap was perched on her head, with a thick, snow-white braid poking out the hole in the back and hanging down over one shoulder. She appeared to be in her eighties.

"I'm sorry," Willow said, thinking she must want to get into the building. "Are we blocking your way?"

"Oh, heavens, no, child. I usually go through the courtyard gate around the other side of the building after my morning walk." She waved one fragile, blue-veined hand to indicate the general direction. "That way I do not have to remember to carry my key. But I saw you here, pushing the manager's buzzer, and I thought I should tell you that he is probably not back yet. He was just leaving the building—a trip to the hardware store, I believe—when I started out on my walk this morning." She gave them a cheery, unabashedly inquisitive smile. "Did you want to see him about renting an apartment?"

Steve shook his head. "We just have a few questions about some former tenants we hoped he might be able to answer. It all depends on how long he's been the manager here."

"Oh, Mr. Amberson has been with the Bachelor Arms for . . ." she tilted her head as she thought about it ". . . for almost twenty-seven years, I believe it has been."

Steve and Willow exchanged a significant glance. Twenty-seven years! This Amberson might be able to tell them something about her mother.

"Yes, I am sure of it," the beautiful old lady said. "He started to work here in 1968. I remember it very well because that was the year I had my apartment painted in shades of mauve. What an unfortunate mistake *that* was," she confided with a lilting laugh that wouldn't have sounded out of place coming from a young girl. "I had Mr. Amberson repaint the entire apartment over for me immediately."

"Then you've been here since 1968, too?" Willow asked, hoping for yet another possible source of information about the mother she'd never known.

"Oh, my dear child, heavens no. I have been a resident of the Bachelor Arms since 1947."

A moment of stunned silence greeted her announcement.

"This has all been way too easy," Steve said. "It's almost scary, it's been so easy. Everything's just been falling into place as if it were meant to be."

"Perhaps the lady in the mirror has something do with it," the tiny woman suggested.

"The lady in the mirror?" Willow asked.

The woman inclined her head toward the brass plaque on the wall. "'Believe the legend,'" she quoted.

"What legend?" Steve demanded, his tone a shade peremptory. Willow nudged him with her elbow, giving him a disapproving little shake of her head when he turned to look down at her. He glanced at the little woman in the pink jogging suit. "What's this legend about?" he asked again, making it a request this time, rather than a demand.

"It's quite a long story," the woman replied. "Please, come to my apartment," she invited them, "and we can all have a nice glass of tea while I tell you about it." She held her hand out, the gesture as gracefully elegant as if they had just been introduced at a ball. "I am Natasha Kuryan."

"Steve Hart." He reached out to take her offered hand as he spoke, carefully enclosing it in his oversize palm. "And this is Willow Ryan. We're both very pleased to meet you, Ms. Kuryan." And then, without thinking, he lifted her hand to his lips and placed a kiss on her fragile fingertips; it seemed to be the only appropriate response to the way she had presented it to him.

Natasha Kuryan's green eyes beamed her approval. "The young people here call me Madame," she said regally. "You may do the same."

"ALTHOUGH THERE ARE many rumors, the true identity of the lady in the mirror is not known," Madame Kuryan said as she poured a small amount of strong black tea into each of three small glasses fitted into silver filigree holders. "She is said to have lived here in the 1920s when the Bachelor Arms was still a magnificent private residence but how the poor lady died remains a mystery." She added hot water to each glass from the ornate brass samovar sitting on the small lace-draped table beside her chair, handing them to her guests as each one was filled.

Steve accepted his a little awkwardly, holding the whole thing, saucer and all, cradled in his palm. He looked distinctly uncomfortable sitting on Madame Kuryan's shawl-draped, red velvet settee, surrounded by lace-covered tables and delicate china bric-a-brac. Willow watched him from under her lashes, smiling when he lifted the tea glass by the rim to drink because his finger wouldn't fit through the delicate silver handle. He glanced up over the edge of the glass as he sipped, catching Willow grinning at him, and gave her a dirty look.

"According to the legend, the circumstances of her death were deeply tragic," Natasha said, unaware of—or ignoring—the byplay between her guests. "She is said to haunt the mirror in apartment 1-G, revealing herself only infrequently. And then only to someone whose life is about to change in some significant way. Her appearance foretells the attainment of your greatest dream or predicts the occasion when your greatest fear will come to pass. A young actress named Jeannie Masters is commonly believed to be the first victim of the mirror. She was found dead in the swimming pool that used to be in the courtyard." Natasha Kuryan slanted a glance across her teacup at Steve. "I see by your expression you do not believe it."

"No offense to you, Madame Kuryan, but it sounds like a load of bull . . . ah, manure to me."

"And if I told you that I, myself, have seen the lady? It was on the very night Errol Flynn and I became lovers."

"And was that the attainment of your greatest dream or the occasion of your deepest fear?" he asked, deadpan.

Natasha Kuryan let out a peal of delighted laughter and shook her head at him. "A lady does not kiss and tell," she admonished him.

"THESE GIRLS, they did not live here long, I think," Natasha said as she looked at the pictures Willow had handed to her after the tea and tiny almond cakes had been set aside. "A month." She shrugged. "Maybe two. But this one, yes." She tapped her finger against Donna Ryan's smiling face. "I remember her very well. A great beauty. Superb bones. I was a makeup artist for many, many years with Xanadu Studios," she told them proudly, "so I know how important good bones are for true beauty. All of the young men in the building pursued her from the day she and the other girl moved into Bachelor Arms." Natasha glanced up, her sharp green eyes narrowing as she stared into Willow's face. "You have a bit of her look around the eyes, although the angle is not so sharp."

"She was my mother."

Natasha Kuryan nodded, as if that explained something she'd been wondering about.

"Do you happen to remember whether she dated anyone in particular while she lived here?" Willow asked. "Anyone in these pictures?"

"Ah, back then, who could tell?" Natasha shrugged and rolled her eyes. "There was all that ridiculous talk of free love and sexual liberation. I saw her with all these young men at one time or another, but to say she was the special sweetheart of any one of them . . . ? I could not even begin to guess."

"What about the guys in the pictures?" Steve urged. "Do you remember anything about any of them?"

"Oh, my heavens, yes," Natasha said. "I remember these young men very well. Very well, indeed. This one with the dashing mustache is Ethan." She sighed and pressed her lips together. "He was not my favorite of the boys."

"Oh?" Steve said encouragingly.

"Too arrogant and full of himself. A failing of many young men, I'm afraid." She looked up, giving Steve a teasing smile. "But perhaps *he* grew out of it."

He smiled in silent acknowledgment of her gentle gibe. "And the others?"

"These two, here, they were brothers," she said, pointing them out as she spoke. "This one is Jack. He was the younger. And this one—" The bright light in her eyes dimmed slightly for a moment. "This one is Eric."

Steve and Willow sought each other's eyes over the old woman's head. Eric? Another man with the initial *E* to add to the mystery surrounding her mother?

"He is dead now," Natasha said sadly. "A suicide, the police said, but I was never convinced of that. I have always preferred to believe it was an unfortunate accident. Although . . . there *was* talk that he had seen the lady in the mirror, so perhaps the police were right."

"Suicide?" Willow echoed, struggling to keep the disappointment out of her voice. "When?"

"Not long after these pictures were taken, I should think. It happened in the summer of 1970. In June. Or perhaps it was July." She shook her head. "My memory is not so good as it once was. You should ask Mr. Amberson if it is important that you know about this. Or, perhaps, you could contact young Jack Shannon. I'm sure Mr. Amberson could give you his forwarding address."

"I doubt any forwarding address he might have would be any good after all this time," Steve said.

"But it has only been a few months since young Jack and his new bride moved out of apartment 1-G. I am quite sure Mr. Amberson will know where they have gone."

"A few months? You mean he's been living here for the last twenty-five years?"

"Oh, no. No, a few months only. He went away after his brother died. It is rumored that he joined the army for a time and then roamed the world trying to forget. It was the lady in the mirror who drew him back. She knew he needed to be here to attain his dream." She looked down at the photographs in her hands. "As did Ezekiel," she said, running her fingertip over the youthful face of Zeke Blackstone. "He had lost his dream, too, and needed to come back to the Bachelor Arms to regain it."

"Now let me get this straight," Steve said. "Are you telling me both those guys have been back here in the last— Did you say *Ezekiel?*"

Natasha nodded. "It is his given name. He admitted it to me one afternoon when he was feeling a little homesick for his mother, soon after he came out here from New York to be a movie star. She was the only one who called him by his true name and he missed hearing it, I think." She smiled a little at the memory. "I thought it a charming name for a charming young man. A little old-fashioned, perhaps, but so much more melodious than Zeke, don't you think?"

4

"*THREE* OF THEM", Willow said. Three of them with the initial *E*. And all of them knew my mother at the right time. All of them may have dated her. Which means any one of them could be my father." She looked up at Steve. "What do we do now?"

"We talk to the manager," Steve said, "and see if he can add anything to what Madame Kuryan told us."

He put his hand under her elbow again, politely ushering her across the pebbled concrete surface of the courtyard. Natasha Kuryan had told them that if Ken Amberson was back from his errand at the hardware store, they would most likely find him in apartment 1-G. There had been a persistent leak in one of the bathroom faucets.

"It is across the courtyard and through the door on the other side," she'd said as she escorted them out of her cozy potpourri-scented apartment. "One-G is the third door on your left after you enter the hallway."

They found it easily enough. The door was standing half-open, the sounds of metal clanging against metal reverberating into the hall. Steve pushed the door all the way open and stepped back, letting Willow enter ahead of him. They walked down a short hallway and into an empty, airy room. The walls were painted a soft, creamy white. Two tall arched windows, flanked by open slatted wooden shutters, spilled long lozenges of sunlight across the floor. A large mirror, easily four feet wide by five feet high, hung on one wall.

It had a heavy ornate pewter frame, distinctively Victorian and elaborately cast with dozens of roses and twining ribbons. It should have looked out of place in the elegant simplicity of the room but, somehow, it didn't.

"Do you think that's the mirror?" Willow whispered.

"Must be. It's the only one in here."

Willow hesitated for a moment, then walked over and stood directly in front of the mirror. There was nothing looking back at her but her own reflection—and then Steve's, as he came up behind her. They were a study in contrasts. He was so big and blond and masculine, with a sexy, laid-back Southern California style that suited him right town to the size-twelve Reeboks on his feet. She was slender and dark, a sleek, sophisticated woman in expensive, tailored clothes.

She had never thought of herself as particularly feminine or fragile—certainly no more so than the average woman—but she looked both standing next to him. It wasn't his height, because he wasn't overpoweringly tall; in her heels, the top of her head came to his nose. It wasn't his physique, either; although that was impressive, his muscles weren't the bulked-up kind so beloved by weight lifters. It was his basic, elemental maleness that made him look so solid and bigger than life. He was totally, unapologetically masculine and he made her feel totally feminine in return. She wasn't quite sure she liked the feeling; it didn't fit in with her image of herself as a modern woman of the world. Willow Ryan didn't lean on anybody, and Steve Hart had shoulders tailor-made for leaning on. Her head had been tilting toward them from the minute she turned her problem over to his capable hands.

"See anything in there?" he asked, leaning forward to whisper the words in her ear.

"No," she murmured and moved away from the mirror. And him. "The banging's stopped," she said, as if he couldn't hear it for himself. "Don't you think we'd better let this Mr. Amberson know we're here so we can ask our questions?"

But Amberson came out of the bathroom before either of them could move to make their presence known. He was a small man, wiry looking, with a shining bald head and a belligerent expression in his pale gray eyes. He was wearing faded green coveralls and carried a length of pipe in his hand. Willow took an instant aversion to him.

"Who're you?" he demanded, looking back and forth between the two of them. "What are you doing in here? This apartment ain't for rent right now."

Willow took a step back, unconsciously edging closer to Steve, more than willing to let him handle the manager of the Bachelor Arms. She'd worry about standing on her own two feet later.

"We're not here to rent an apartment," Steve said. "We'd just like to ask you a few questions."

"You reporters?"

"No, we're—"

"Been a lot of reporters nosin' around here ever since it leaked out about Blackstone renting this place. Damned bloodsucking nuisances, every one of them. Well, he's gone," he said, gesturing at the empty room with the piece of pipe he held in his hand. "Left last month, right after his kid's wedding. So if you're working for one of them tabloids or that 'Hard Copy' program, you can get the hell out of here, right now. I ain't got nothin' to say."

"We're not reporters, Mr. Amberson," Steve assured him. He reached into the back pocket of his jeans and pulled out his wallet. "I'm a private investigator." He extracted a business card and handed it to Amberson. "Ms. Ryan is my client."

Amberson studied the card for a moment. "What are you investigating?"

"Zeke Blackstone, for starters," Steve said.

"I knew you was a couple of reporters," Amberson said angrily. He tossed the card on the floor in disgust and started to turn away. "Get outta here before I call the cops."

"And Ethan Roberts," Steve said.

Amberson turned back around to face them. "Huh?"

"And Eric and Jack Shannon," Steve added softly, knowing he had him now by the suddenly avid look in the smaller man's eyes. "And their possible connection to a young woman by the name of Donna Ryan."

"Where'd you get them names?"

Steve glanced at Willow, silently indicating the pictures she carried in her pocket. Intuitively understanding his intent, she withdrew all eight and handed them to him. Steve sorted through them quickly, selected the one he wanted, and handed it to Amberson.

The older man was silent for a long minute, studying the picture in his hand. "You want to know about the suicide, don'cha?"

"We want to know about that summer," Steve said. "Whatever you remember."

"Why?"

"The reason is confidential."

"Then so's my memory."

Steve flipped his wallet open again. "Would twenty dollars help make it less so?"

Amberson didn't so much as glance at the money.

"Forty?"

Willow reached out and put her hand on Steve's arm. "Mr. Amberson isn't interested in your money," she said. She didn't know how she knew that, but she did. The covetous look in his strange gray eyes wasn't for the greenbacks in Steve's wallet but for the secrets of other people's lives. Amberson wouldn't take money for what he knew but he would trade information for information.

"Donna Ryan was my mother," Willow said to him. "We think one of the men in that picture is my father."

"YEAH, I REMEMBER HER. She was a real looker," Amberson said. "Moved in here with her girlfriend back in May of 1970. Ethan Roberts—the one who's running for senator now—he was the one who told her about the vacant apartment. He was working with her on some TV program . . . some soap opera thing. Guess he thought he'd have a better chance to score with her if she was close by."

"And did he?" Steve asked.

"Who the hell knows?" Amberson shrugged. "It was wild around here in those days. Parties all the time. Kids climbing in an' out of each other's beds like they was playing a game of musical chairs. Didn't have no AIDS to worry about back then. I know she went out with Roberts a couple a times. But I seen her go out with other guys, too, including Eric Shannon. You ask me whether she was sleeping with any of them, I got to be honest and tell you I don't know. She didn't let none of the guys crawl all over her like some of the girls did. Leastways, not in public so's anyone could watch it."

He pushed open the door to the courtyard and stepped outside. Steve stuck his hand out over Willow's shoulder, stopping the heavy door with his palm before it could close in her face.

"Now, right here is where Blackstone stumbled over the body that night," Amberson said with relish, pointing to a spot on the concrete courtyard patio where a tub of flowering hibiscus now stood. "The police said the Shannon kid had been dead for a couple of hours by the time Blackstone fell over him. Couple a people actually walked around him while he was lying there like that, thinking he was just was passed out drunk or on drugs or something. Two kids was lying on a chaise longue right over there, makin' out, and they didn't even notice him. He'd landed on his back, smashed in his skull real good and broke his spine in three places, but you couldn't tell that by just looking at him. And it was dark. With the shadows and everything, nobody noticed the blood."

He seemed to derive a macabre sort of enjoyment from being the teller of the sad tale. Like an ugly little troll, Willow thought, dispensing his horrid little gems, one by one, and watching to see how they would be accepted.

"Cops figure he jumped from the third floor. From that balcony up there," he said as he pointed it out. He looked straight at Willow. "That's where your mother and her girlfriend lived," he said, watching her for a reaction.

"He jumped from my mother's apartment?" She felt Steve's hands settle on her shoulders from behind. They steadied her in some indefinable way, transferring his strength into her just when she needed it most. "Was she there when it happened?" she asked calmly. "Did she see him jump?"

Amberson shook his head. "Cops figure she was down at the party in 1-G when it happened. She was the one who heard the screaming, though. Called the ambulance, too."

"There was screaming?" Willow said. "I thought you said no one saw what happened."

"Girl on the chaise longue with her boyfriend started screeching when she realized they'd been doin' the nasty in front of a dead body." Amberson rubbed his chin with the back of the hand that still held the pipe. "Didn't seem to bother her none when she thought he was just drunk."

"What was he doing in Donna's apartment if she wasn't there?" Steve asked, steering the conversation back to what he considered a more relevant topic. "How'd he get in?"

"All he'd a had to do was open the door and walk in. Like I said, it was pretty free and easy here in those days. Nobody bothered much with locking anything up. Cops figured he probably chose her apartment because he knew no one was there to stop him from killin' himself."

Willow was silent a moment, contemplating that, trying to gather her thoughts, trying to sort out how she would feel if Eric Shannon turned out to be her father—and she'd lost him before she even found him. "Does anybody know *why* he killed himself?" she asked.

"There was some talk about him and his brother having a big argument that night but, hell, who knows? Could be true, I guess. The two of 'em were always arguing over something, and Jack Shannon did disappear right after the inquest, which kinda points to a guilty conscience, if you ask me. He ended up in 'Nam and then became one of them mercenaries you read about. Traveled all over the world, selling his services to the highest bidder. 'Course—" Amberson shrugged "—could be there wasn't no argument at all. Could be Eric Shannon was just so loaded he thought he could fly. It don't make any difference why, anyway. It had to happen."

"*Had* to happen?" Steve said.

"He saw the woman in the mirror."

"The legend again," Steve said. "That's a load of crap and you know it."

"The legend's true," Amberson said stubbornly. "Back in 1930 an actress named Jeannie Masters drowned in the swimming pool that used to be right here where we're standing. You can see the outline of it," he said, pointing. "It happened during a wild party, just like with the Shannon kid, and nobody saw a thing. Nobody knows whether it was an accident or suicide or murder."

"Oh, for cryin' out loud," Steve said, all but throwing his hands up in exasperation. "That story is nothing but a bunch of superstitious mumbo jumbo dreamed up by somebody with more imagination than sense—probably in an effort to attract tenants to this place."

"It's as true as I'm standing here," Amberson insisted. "She appears in the mirror in 1-G in a long white dress and smiles, sorta sadlike, and then you know something is gonna happen."

"You're telling us that you've actually seen this mysterious ghost woman?"

"I ain't saying I have and I ain't saying I haven't. I'm just saying I know what happens to people who do."

"Yeah, right," Steve scoffed. "And the only ones who've ever seen her are a select group of stiffs and a sweet little old lady with romantic memories."

"Madame ain't the only one who's seen her and lived to tell about it," Amberson said angrily. "Ethan Roberts saw her the same day he got his big break on the soap opera. And Jack Shannon's wife saw her, too, first time she was ever in the apartment."

"WE'RE ALL SET for tonight." Steve flipped his cellular phone closed with a quick flick of his wrist and slid it into the inside pocket of his sport coat. "We're meeting Jack Shannon and his wife right over there—" he pointed at the brick-fronted building next to the Bachelor Arms "—at Flynn's." He reached for the key dangling in the ignition of the Mustang. "Six o'clock, or as soon after that as traffic permits."

"Okay." Willow nodded her head in agreement. "Sounds good."

But something in her voice didn't sound good at all. He released the key without firing the ignition. "You doin' okay over there, sweetheart?" he asked softly, without a trace of his teasing Bogart voice. He reached out to tuck an errant lock of hair behind her ear. "You look a little shell-shocked."

Willow leaned into his touch, for just a second, as his fingers brushed the side of her face—and then tilted her head away, quickly, before she could give in to the urge to rub her cheek against his big, warm palm. "I'm fine," she said.

Steve let his hand fall to the curve of her neck. "It's a big adjustment to go from having no idea who your father is to finding out there's a good chance he might be any one of three men, all in one morning," he said, kneading gently. "Nobody would blame you for feeling a little overwhelmed."

"I'm fine," she said again, shooting him a wary glance. "Really. I'm not one of those delicate flowers who falls apart over the least little thing." At least, she hadn't been until this morning. "You don't need to worry that I'll start sniveling all over you again. I promise, I won't."

The corner of Steve's beautifully chiseled mouth quirked up in an amused little grin. "No need to be embarrassed, sweetheart." The Bogie imitation was back. "You can snivel all over me anytime you need to. It's included in my hourly fee."

"Does that hourly fee include stud service, too?" she snapped and then gasped at the look that crossed his face.

She didn't know what had made her say it, she really didn't, except that if he didn't stop touching her neck like that she was going to climb over the gearshift and crawl into his lap.

He dropped his hand from her neck. "If you're worried about what happened in my office this morning, don't be. It was a pathetic lack of control on my part," he admitted, "and I sincerely apologize for it."

"Apologize for what?" she asked, wondering what on earth he thought he had to apologize for. He had kissed her, that's all, offering comfort when she needed it.

"For taking advantage of you when you were in an emotionally vulnerable state."

"Taking advantage of me?" she said, insulted. Nobody took advantage of Willow Ryan. She didn't permit it.

"As long as you're my client you don't have to worry about my intentions," he said, stating it as plainly as he knew how. If he was going to help her, she had to trust him. And she couldn't trust him if she was afraid he was going to jump her any second. "I don't have sex with my clients."

Willow couldn't believe what she was hearing. "And just what makes you think you had the *slightest* chance of having sex with me?" she demanded acidly.

"There was no thinking involved, sweetheart. Not by me and not by you. If I'd wanted to, I could have had you this morning, buck naked and screaming with pleasure on the couch in my office. And we both know it."

Willow just stared at him with her mouth hanging inelegantly open, speechless in front of such unmitigated masculine arrogance.

"And just for the record, sweetheart . . . When this is all over and we've found out who your daddy is, that's just what I'm going to do."

5

WILLOW DID SOMETHING that afternoon that she'd never done before. She canceled two business appointments and went shopping instead. Steve was picking her up at her hotel at five-thirty to meet the Shannons at Flynn's by six and there was a lot to do before she would be ready for him.

She still couldn't believe the unmitigated, colossal gall of the man. The sheer arrogance of his attitude.

So, okay, she'd responded to his kisses with a certain amount of warmth. Big deal. She'd been upset, taken off guard; he'd been right about that. But it certainly didn't mean she wanted to go to bed with him. To lie down on that ratty leather sofa in his office "buck naked and screaming with pleasure," as he had so crudely put it.

An image of that happening flickered through her mind: all those rippling muscles, taut and trembling under her caressing fingertips; those big warm hands on her thighs; his golden body all naked and aroused, slick with passion as he worked over her. In her. Heat flooded her body.

Well, okay, maybe she wouldn't mind it all that much . . . under the right circumstances . . . if he asked nicely.

But for him to say, flat out, that he could have her any time he wanted . . . that he *intended* to have her as soon as it suited some outdated, antiquated notions of his, and never mind what she thought about it . . .

"We'll just see about that," she muttered, slamming the door to her hotel room as she headed out to hit the stores on Rodeo Drive. "By the time I get through with you, Steve Hart, you'll be on your knees, begging me to put you out of your misery."

SHE WAS DRESSED all in black when he picked her up at her hotel that evening. Black heels, black stockings, a snug little black dinner suit with a high, round collar and long, fitted jacket that showed off her slim figure.

And she had a great little figure to show off, Steve thought appreciatively, eyeing her through the windshield as he pulled his Mustang into the porticoed driveway of the hotel. Her tailored business suit hadn't shown the half of it. Which, he supposed, was the purpose of a business suit.

He wondered why she was outside, chatting with the doorman, instead of waiting inside for him. It offended his sense of chivalry to see her standing there on the curb. He would have let the valet stand watch over his car while he went in and got her. As it was, she didn't even give him a chance to get out and open the door for her. She reached for it herself as soon as he pulled to a stop, yanked it open, and slid into the front seat, waving a cheery goodbye to the doorman as they left.

"So, what did you find out from your police buddy?" she asked, crossing her legs as she settled back against the white leather. Her black skirt slid halfway up her thighs with the movement, showing off a spectacular pair of legs.

Steve glanced at her face, wondering if she'd exposed that silky length of stocking-covered thigh on purpose, as a way to get back at him for being, as she'd so delicately put it when she'd slammed his car door, "an arrogant ass."

Willow looked back at him with a bland smile, one eyebrow raised slightly, waiting for an answer to her question. "Well, what did he say?" she asked.

He supposed it could have been unintentional. The skirt, unlike the gray pin-striped one she'd had on earlier, was quite narrow. There was no place for it to go but up when she crossed her legs. He decided to give her the benefit of the doubt.

"Marty confirmed what Amberson told us. Eric Shannon jumped—or fell—to his death from the third-floor apartment of Donna Ryan and Christine Loudon, her roommate. No one saw him do it. No one knows why he did it. The closest anyone could come to a reason was the argument he'd had with his brother but even the cops thought that was pretty thin. He wasn't as loaded as Amberson implied, either. The autopsy revealed blood alcohol levels equivalent to a couple of beers, and there was some trace evidence of marijuana use. But nothing more than that. So it's highly unlikely he flung himself over the railing in some kind of drug-induced frenzy." He slanted a glance at her, wanting to see how she'd take the next bit of information. "It happened on June 28th, 1970. Almost eight months to the day from the date you were born."

"Does that make it more or less likely that he's the one?"

"It makes it *possible*," Steve said. "No more, no less."

"So we still have three possibles, then." She sighed, loudly, her bottom lip pushed out in a disappointed little pout, and recrossed her legs. The skirt inched a few crucial inches higher. "Were you able to find out anything from anyone on that soap opera my mother was on?"

"Nothing really helpful. You knew it was a long shot," he said, wondering when in hell she was going to pull that skirt down. She'd smoothed her other, longer skirt down over her thighs a half-dozen times that day. "There aren't many of the same people working on a soap opera after twenty-five years but I was able to convince the secretary in the studio office to dig through some of their old records for me."

I'll just bet you did, Willow fumed, and lifted her hand to her throat.

"I was able to confirm the dates both Donna Ryan and Ethan Roberts worked there. They overlapped but we already knew they would. A couple of the older actors remembered working with her. One of them said he'd thought she'd had some real talent, and had always wondered why she'd left the show, especially when the writers were making plans to beef up her part.

A makeup artist recognized her picture right off the bat, and for the same reason Madame Kuryan did," he said, sliding her another glance out of the corner of his eye. "Superb bone struct— What are you doing?"

"I shouldn't have worn such a heavy suit." Her long slim fingers were halfway down the front of her jacket, her shiny red fingertips sliding in and out of the hidden placket as she worked each button loose. "Especially not one with such a high, constricting collar."

Steve found his eyes glued to those red nails. Had they been that color earlier today? And wouldn't he have noticed if they had been?

"Look out for that car up ahead," Willow warned him. "The light's about to turn red."

He jerked his gaze back to the road just in time to avoid plowing into the car in front of him. With the Mustang safely stopped at the light, he turned his head back toward Willow, his mouth half-open to continue his report—and almost swallowed his tongue.

She was leaning forward in her seat, trying to shimmy out of the tight-fitting jacket. The creamy mounds of her breasts were practically spilling out over the low, square-cut bodice of the little black dress she wore under it.

"Could you help me with this, please?" she asked, extending her left arm out to him so he could pull the cuff off over her hand.

Speechless, his gaze glued to the quivering mounds of her breasts, he did as she asked.

"Thank you." She gave him a polite little smile. "I didn't expect it to still be this warm in October," she said as she wriggled the rest of the way out of the jacket. "This is the only evening outfit I brought with me, so I didn't have a choice about what to wear."

It was a blatant, bald-faced lie. She'd bought the outfit that afternoon at Gianni Versace's Rodeo Drive boutique, right after she'd gotten her hair and nails done at Vidal Sassoon.

"The light's green," she said, hiding a satisfied smile as she carefully folded the jacket. Knowing he was watching out of the corner of his eye, she shifted around, wriggling a good bit more than necessary, and draped it over the back of her seat. Then, settling back down, she lifted both hands and ran her fingers up through the back of her hair to fluff it. The movement lifted her breasts even higher, threatening indecent exposure if she wasn't careful.

Steve's hands began to sweat against the leather-wrapped steering wheel. "Just what in the hell do you think you're doing?" he growled through clenched teeth.

Willow dropped her arms. "Doing?" she said innocently, turning her head to look him full in the face.

"Don't bothering giving me that wide-eyed look," he warned her. "I know when a woman's up to no good."

She hooked a sheaf of hair behind her ear with one long red fingernail. "I don't know *what* you're talking about."

He had to admire her nerve; most people backed down when he growled at them like that. She just shrugged and gave him her shoulder. Her soft, bare, creamy, sexy shoulder.

"Isn't that Flynn's?" she said, pointing as they passed it.

Steve swore and made an illegal U-turn, causing her to reach out and brace herself against the dashboard.

"That wasn't very nice," she said, shooting him a pouty look as she straightened. "I could have broken a nail."

"Keep it up and it might be your neck," he warned as he nosed the car into a parking space beside Flynn's.

He cut the engine and then sat there a minute, his hands on the steering wheel as he struggled to get control of his rampaging libido. Why did women always use sex when they wanted to get even with a man? Didn't they know the kind of trouble it could get them into? He was as hard as a rock, and about two seconds away from dragging her into the back seat and peeling her out of that dress. Only the fact that she was his client kept him from acting on the impulse.

He loosened his grip on the steering wheel and turned to face her, prepared to calmly, concisely and in terms guaranteed to blister her pretty little ears, tell her exactly what he thought of the ridiculous game she was playing. "Do you have any idea how close you came?"

"Hmm?" she murmured absently, unconcernedly rummaging through a tiny, beaded black evening bag.

She extracted a tube of lipstick and reached for the rearview mirror. "Do you mind?" she said, twisting it around to face her without waiting for his consent.

"Willow," he said, his voice low and threatening. And laced with willing laughter. He was having a hard time maintaining any kind of righteous male anger in the face of her determined indifference to it.

"Yes, go ahead. I'm listening," she said, as she began carefully applying a fresh coat of red lipstick. She made a production of it, parting her lips in a sexy pout, slowly drawing the tube of color over them. "I have no idea how close I came to . . . ?" she prompted, urging him to complete the thought.

Steve couldn't help it. He laughed. "Are you trying to drive me *completely* around the bend?"

"Yes." She gave him a saucy smile as she put the lid back on her lipstick. "How am I doing?"

"I'm halfway there already," he admitted. "I was halfway there when you crossed your legs. And you know it, you heartless little witch."

"Good." She dropped the lipstick in her purse and snapped the tiny bag shut. "You deserved it."

Steve shook his head in exasperation. Only a woman would punish a man for trying to save her from his baser instincts. The whole female sex was crazy, and men were crazy for putting up with their nonsense— and coming back for more with their tongues hanging out.

"You stay right there until I come around and open that door," he said as she reached for the car's door handle. "The pavement in this parking lot is full of potholes. You could break your neck."

"Before you could break it for me, you mean?"

"You've got a real sassy mouth on you," he said as he opened the car door. "I don't know why I didn't notice it before."

"Probably because you were staring at my chest."

He gave her a narrowed look as he extended his hand to her. "Sooner or later," he warned her, "that mouth's gonna get you in a whole lot of trouble."

She pursed her shiny red lips at him in an exaggerated kissing motion. "Promises, promises," she taunted and, placing her hand in his, swung her legs out of the car, giving him plenty of time to ogle them while she did so.

And he did, blatantly, letting his gaze travel from the thigh-high hem of her dress to the impossibly high heels on her feet. The muscles in his stomach tensed as if he'd just taken a punch to the gut. How the hell had she known?

Her damned shoes were straight out of his fantasies, made of narrow black velvet straps and black satin ribbons that tied in neat little bows around her slender ankles. Steve took a deep breath and decided, then and there, that the first time he made love to her she was going to be wearing those shoes—and nothing else.

"Oh, grab my jacket for me, will you?" she said, brushing past him while he stood there, thinking about all the things he meant to do to her when he got her in his bed. "Sometimes the air-conditioning can be a bit chilly."

She strolled on toward Flynn's ahead of him, her hips swaying lazily as she silently fired another salvo in their delicious little battle of the sexes.

"*Good God Almighty, woman,*" she heard him rasp hoarsely, and she knew she'd hit her mark.

The back of the dress was cut past discretion, coming to a V just below the curve of her waist. Her black stockings were seamed. The poor sap didn't have a chance.

"I'll get even with you for this," he growled, his voice laced with amused frustration.

Willow laughed and kept on walking. "You're certainly welcome to try," she taunted.

FLYNN'S WAS A NICE little neighborhood bar, with a black-and-white art decoish decor that made it elegant and cozy at the same time. Vintage posters from old Errol Flynn movies decorated the walls, interspersed with glossy publicity photos of some of the biggest stars from Hollywood's Golden Era. Waitresses clad in modified, skirted tuxedos with jaunty red bow ties moved deftly through the noisy, cheerful crowd, dispensing drinks, high-calorie munchies and the occasional wisecrack. Happy Hour was in full swing.

Willow realized immediately that she was overdressed—or underdressed, depending on how you looked at it—for the Friday-night after-work crowd. Two yuppie business types at a nearby table stopped talking to stare at her exposed cleavage, one of the waitresses gave her a sliding sideways glance, and a distinguished, extremely well-dressed man with a small brown mustache raised his wineglass and winked appreciatively.

Willow had a moment of uneasiness at the attention she was attracting, wondering if there was a way to make a graceful retreat, when she heard a threatening growl rumble in her ear.

"Here, put this on, dammit," Steve said, draping her jacket around her from behind.

The man with the wine blanched and looked away, the two yuppies abruptly returned to their conversation. Willow turned her head, looking over her shoulder to see what Steve had done to cause the men's sudden disinterest in her charms.

He was standing behind her with his hands on her shoulders, like an alpha wolf standing guard over a juicy little rabbit, warning any and all comers he wouldn't hesitate to tear them apart if they dared to challenge his right to it. The look in his eyes sent shivers of delicious fear and excitement racing down Willow's spine.

She hadn't counted on arousing his jealousy; she hadn't even considered it as an option when she started her teasing little game. She should have, she realized now. Steve Hart was all man. Men were notoriously territorial by nature, and she forgot all about being overdressed for the occasion and began wondering just how far she could exploit this unlooked-for bonus without taking it too far and getting herself—or anyone else—into serious trouble.

"Don't even think about it," Steve said, bending his head to whisper the words into her ear. "You wouldn't like it if one of these slobbering Romeos got hurt because you were trying to bring me to heel." He turned her around to face him. "You want to yank on my chain a little more, fine. But this is between you and me, sweetheart. Let's keep it that way."

He bent down and pressed a hard, possessive kiss on her astonished mouth, then whirled her around again and, hands firmly on her shoulders, headed her through the Happy Hour crowd toward the bar.

"Which one of you is Eddie?" he asked, aiming his question at the two bartenders working behind the long polished bar.

"That'd be me," answered the one dispensing beer into a frosted pilsner glass. He took a moment to set the drink down on a napkin in front of his customer before turning his attention to Steve. "What can I do for you?"

"I'm supposed to be meeting a man by the name of Jack Shannon in here tonight. He said you could point him out for me."

"Sure thing," Eddie said easily, making a credible effort not to let his gaze stray toward Willow's enticing cleavage. "He's sitting right over there, in that first booth, with his wife, Faith."

"Thanks." Steve reached over Willow's shoulder and laid a couple of bills on the bar. "Have somebody bring a couple of drinks over to the table, would you please. I'll have a beer—whatever you have on tap. Willow?"

"Tequila shooter," Willow said, just to annoy him. She smiled at the bartender as if he were the best-looking man she'd ever seen in her life. "You can keep them coming until I start to dance on the tables."

Steve slid his hand from her shoulder to the back of her neck and squeezed gently. "Just bring her a margarita," he said to the bartender.

"Frozen. No salt," Willow added as he steered her away from the bar with the hand on the back of her neck.

"You can let go of me any time now," she snapped at him as they threaded their way through the crowd to the booths along the wall.

"Are you going to behave yourself?"

"Define *behave*," she retorted.

"Willow . . ." he said warningly and tightened his hand.

"All right, all right. No need to get rough." She gave an exaggerated wince, as if he had actually hurt her when, in truth, he hadn't hurt her at all. "I'll behave."

He let go of her neck.

"But only because I wouldn't want to be responsible for a bar brawl," she added, shooting him a venomous glare to show him she wasn't completely cowed.

He grinned at her. "God, you're a piece of work," he said admiringly.

Willow bent her head, refusing to let him see her smile, and dug into her evening bag. "Here," she said and handed him a tissue. "Wipe your mouth off. You've got lipstick all over it."

JACK SHANNON WAS a good twenty years older than his wife. Faith was about Willow's age, with pale brown hair that fell to her shoulders in a soft wave, big hazel eyes and a face as fresh and innocent as an angel's. It was a situation that would have normally made Willow think snidely of middle-aged men desperately trying to hang on to their youth, except that there was nothing desperate or middle-aged about Jack Shannon. He could very easily have been the mercenary Amberson had accused him of being. As lean and rangy as a hungry panther, with a panther's watchful eyes and coiled readiness, he looked as if he were ready to spring into explosive action at the first sign of danger. Willow had no trouble at all picturing him slogging through a South American jungle or slinking across a foreign desert with an Uzi slung over his shoulder, recovered government secrets in his pack and an enemy camp exploding in the darkness behind him . . . except when he looked at his lovely young wife and every bit of hardness and suspicion faded from his eyes.

"Yes, I remember her," he said, looking down at the photographs Steve had spread out on the table. "These pictures were taken the day she and her roommate moved in. April, I think it was. The four of us helped them get their stuff up to the third floor and then we all sat around the courtyard and had a couple of beers."

"Did she date your brother?" Steve asked.

"Maybe." Jack shrugged. "I kind of had the impression she and Ethan had something going, though. I remember him talking about her when she got that part on 'As Time Goes By'—about what a great-looking babe he thought she was and all—and I seem to recall that he was the one responsible for her moving into the BA in the first place. They went out at least a couple of times that I know of. Ethan made sure everybody knew he was going out with her. But . . ." He shook his head. "I don't know. I *think* she dated Eric, too, although I don't know how serious it was. The two of us were pretty much on the outs that summer, hardly on speaking terms most of the time, so we didn't share a lot of brotherly confidences. If we had, maybe I could have prevented what happened."

Faith Shannon laid her hand over her husband's clenched fist. He immediately turned his hand, palm up on the table, and twined his fingers with hers.

"We argued that night," Jack went on. "It was a stupid argument and I ended up storming out in a rage. I never saw my brother alive again."

"I'm sorry," Willow said, touched by the depths of suffering in his dark eyes. "I wouldn't be asking these questions if it wasn't important."

"Yeah, well . . . water under the bridge and all that," he said, brushing aside her concern. "What's done is done."

"How about Zeke Blackstone?" Steve asked.

"You mean, did he date her? No, I don't think so. He was pretty heavily involved with Ariel Cameron back then. They were shooting a movie together."

"They recently got remarried, didn't they?" Willow asked.

"Yeah." Jack grinned. "Two weeks after their daughter's wedding they eloped to Las Vegas like a couple of kids."

"Do you know why they got divorced in the first place?" Steve asked.

Jack lifted an eloquent eyebrow. "You'd have to ask Zeke about that."

"I intend to," Steve said. "Did you date Donna Ryan?"

"She was way out of my league," Jack said easily. "A gorgeous actress, a good three or four years older than me. I wouldn't have presumed."

"So you didn't date her, then?" Steve insisted, wanting a straight yes-or-no answer.

Jack gave him a look that said he didn't like to be pushed. Steve gave him a look that said he'd keep right on pushing until he got what he wanted.

"No," Jack said flatly. "I didn't date her."

Steve nodded, satisfied with that. "What about the card?" he asked. "Do you recognize the handwriting?"

Jack shook his head. "I wish I could be more helpful but it's been twenty-five years since I've seen anything my brother's written."

"What about that box of stuff Mr. Amberson had in the basement?" Faith Shannon said in her soft Georgia drawl. "The one he gave you when you moved back into the Bachelor Arms? Weren't there some notes and pictures and things of his in there with the script?"

"Yes, I think there were," Jack said, nodding his head in agreement. "I'd forgotten about that box. I think it probably got put in storage with a lot of other stuff when we moved out of the BA."

"Would it be all right . . . could we look through it?" Willow asked eagerly.

"I'd have to find it for you first, but sure. You're welcome to look through it if you think it might help."

"Anything might help," Steve said.

Jack slipped two fingers into the pocket of his khaki shirt and pulled out a card. "That's got both my home number and my desk at the *Times* on it," he said as he handed it across the table. "Give me a call and we'll set something up."

"The *Los Angeles Times*?" Willow said. "You're a reporter, then, not a . . ." Her voice trailed off as she realized what she was about to say.

Jack snorted. "Did Amberson give you that fairy tale about me being a mercenary of some kind?"

"He did mention it," Willow admitted.

"Jack was never a mercenary," Faith said loyally, jumping in to set the record straight before her husband could do it himself. "He was a foreign correspondent for the paper. He covers the city beat now," she added proudly.

"Amberson's a few bricks short of a full load," Jack said as he lifted his wife's hand to his lips for a quick kiss. "Always has been." He quirked a brow at his two questioners. "Did he tell you the story about the legend of Bachelor Arms?"

"In gory detail." Willow shivered. "He seemed to delight in making it sound as gruesome as possible."

"Oh, he does," Jack assured her. "I think he resents never having seen the lady himself, so he dwells on the horror stories instead of the good things that have happened to people."

"Are you saying *you've* seen her?" Steve asked, his tone clearly skeptical.

"It's not something I like to admit in public but, yeah," Jack said. A corner of his mouth turned up in a sheepish smile. "I've seen her." He slanted a glance at his wife, who smiled lovingly back. "We both have."

Steve shook his head in disbelief. "And you a reporter for the *Times*," he scoffed.

"'There are more things in heaven and earth, Horatio,/Than are dreamt of in your philosophy,'" Jack quoted with a shrug. "I can't explain what we saw, or why, or how, but I know we saw it."

Steve looked back and forth between the two of them, taking in the twin expressions of absolute conviction. "You're not kidding, are you? You both really think you saw a ghost."

"We saw something, Mr. Hart," Faith Shannon said, rushing to her husband's defense like Beauty defending the Beast, "and it changed our lives. Personally, I don't care whether it was a ghost, a heavenly spirit or an optical illusion. And I don't care what anyone else thinks about it, either," she said tartly, her expression daring him to make something of it.

"Well, I guess that puts me in my place," Steve said with a grin. "I didn't mean to question your veracity," he apologized.

"Only our common sense, hmm?" Faith quipped, letting him know he was forgiven.

Jack reached out and gathered up the pictures, then paused to study them one more time. "I'd like to be able to say I see a strong resemblance but . . ." He shook his head. "Your hair is the same color Eric's was," he offered.

"The same color yours is," interjected his wife.

"The same color as ten other people in this bar," the ever pragmatic Steve pointed out.

Jack handed the pictures to Willow. "If you'd like, I'd be willing to take a blood test."

"A blood test?" Willow said, startled. "You mean, like DNA? To prove conclusively that you're not my father?"

"To find out if I might be your uncle."

Willow looked at Steve. "Is that possible?" she asked, hope flaring in her eyes. "Are those tests sophisticated enough to prove that kind of relationship?"

"It's possible, I guess," Steve admitted reluctantly, unwilling to raise her hopes before he knew for sure. "I'd have to make a few calls to find out."

"I've already done quite a bit of research on it," Jack told them. "Because of the Simpson trial," he added when Steve shot him a suspicious look over the table.

"With the technology available today it would be possible for a DNA test to prove, with nearly one hundred percent accuracy, that we *aren't* related. On the other hand, it could tell us with eighty percent probability if we *are*." He looked into Willow's eyes. "I'm willing to accept those odds, if you are."

6

WILLOW WAS QUIET when they left Flynn's, mulling over what little Jack Shannon had been able to tell them about the possible identity of her father. They were no closer to an answer than they'd been before but she smiled as she settled into the bucket seat of the Mustang, warmed by Jack Shannon's offer to take a blood test. He seemed to want to find out the truth about her paternity nearly as badly as she did.

"Thinking up more ways to torment me?" Steve asked, giving her a wry, amused glance as he slid behind the wheel of the car.

Willow hadn't been thinking anything of the kind. She'd forgotten all about their private battle of the sexes the minute they sat down across the table from Jack and Faith Shannon—but it only took that one challenging sidelong glance to remind her that she'd meant to bring Steve Hart to his knees.

She turned toward him, her legs crossed, her head tilted back against the white leather seat, a seductive smile curving her red lips, and applied herself to the project with renewed enthusiasm.

"WOULD YOU LIKE TO KISS me good-night?" she murmured seductively as they stood in front of the door to her hotel room later.

Steve shook his head. "I don't think that would be such a good idea," he said with real regret edging the amusement in his voice.

Willow lifted her hand and slowly ran the edge of her tiny evening purse down the middle of his broad chest. "Afraid you won't be able to control yourself?" she challenged him.

"Afraid I won't be able to control you," he countered with a grin, and grabbed her wrist, stopping her descending hand before it reached his belt buckle.

They'd been playing this game all night, through dinner at the little Mexican hole-in-the-wall restaurant he'd taken her to after they'd left Flynn's, through the ride back to the hotel, during the elevator's slow ascent to her floor. She'd teased and taunted him, blatantly flaunting her not-inconsiderable charms, playing the outrageous coquette to his staid and stalwart Dudley Do-Right. And he'd enjoyed every single, maddening minute of it, egging her on with taunts of his own just to see how far she would go in her attempt to win their battle of wills. Much to his delight, she'd gotten bolder as the evening progressed, upping the ante from teasing sidelong glances and deliberate displays of flesh to outright innuendo and fleeting touches that just bordered on being caresses.

But, damn, it was beginning to tell on him!

There was a limit to how long a man could stand being in a constant, unrelieved state of arousal, and he'd just about reached that limit. It was time to call it quits before he did something they'd both regret.

"What do you say we declare a cease-fire?" he suggested, putting his hands on her shoulders to push her away from him.

But Willow wasn't about to abandon the attack while he was still standing. Especially not while he still wore that insufferably smug, amused male grin.

She resisted the pressure of his hands and leaned into him, letting her breasts rest against his chest. "Sure I can't tempt you?" she murmured, looking up at him from under the thick fringe of her lashes.

Steve looked down at the lush expanse of feminine flesh pressed against him. Framed by the edges of her open jacket, the smooth ivory globes of her breasts swelled over the low-cut bodice of her dress in blatant invitation. A tiny muscle began to twitch in his chiseled jaw. The amused grin faded. "You could tempt a saint without half trying," he growled.

Willow smiled and tilted her head back, giving him an even better view. "But not you," she said, pouting.

"But not me," he said stiffly, suddenly wondering how he could ever have thought this little game of hers was the least bit amusing. He was suddenly so hard it hurt. "I don't get sexually involved with my clients," he said through clenched teeth. "It's a rule I have."

Willow lifted her chin so that her lips were mere inches from his. She knew she was playing with fire, she could see it in the blue flames burning in his eyes as he looked at her, feel it in the way his hands flexed against her shoulders, but some devil of feminine pride—or feminine desire—pushed her to test his limits. And her own.

She licked her lips. Slowly. "Is that an ironclad rule?" she murmured.

His mouth suddenly dry, Steve nodded.

She tilted her chin a bit more and ran her free hand up the lapel of his sport jacket to the back of his neck. "Even if you've been specifically invited to break it?" she whispered, her fingers feathering up through his hair.

"Is this a real invitation, Willow?" he murmured, his voice harsh and husky. "Or is this still part of the game?"

"Would you say yes if it was real?"

"Later, when this is over, and you've got your balance again, I'll say yes so fast it'll make your head spin," he promised.

"No. Not later. Now," she said, and went up on tiptoe to press her lips to his.

She felt him stiffen, holding himself back from her kiss. One second . . . two . . . five . . . and then his control broke and his arms came around her, gathering her to him as if he meant to never let her go.

She'd won.

But, suddenly, it wasn't a game anymore.

Fire raced through her. Hot. Heady. Utterly irresistible. She dropped her purse and wrapped both arms around his neck, holding him as tightly as he was holding her. Her mouth opened for his tongue as he plunged it between her lips. Her body softened, melting into his without forethought or calculation, instinctively reacting to his show of masculine aggression with fierce feminine surrender.

He slid his big hands down her back to cup her bottom, pressing her softness into the hardness of his painfully aroused body.

She moaned into his mouth, answering his silent demand with a rolling undulation of her pelvis.

He backed her up against the door of her room, holding her there with the slow, grinding thrust of his hips, and ran his hands up her sides to her breasts.

She arched her back, thrusting them into his hands.

He curled his fingers over the edge of her low-cut bodice, pulled it down, and cupped her bare breasts in his palms.

She gasped, her nipples hardening in instant response.

And then, carefully capturing one pebbled nub between his thumb and forefinger, he bent his head and took the other into his mouth.

Willow cried out as twin bolts of lightning ricocheted through her body. She couldn't tell which pleasure was the greater; his hard, callused fingertips plucking delicately at one rigid nipple, the warmth of his mouth, sucking strongly at the other—or the rock-hard erection pressing against the exquisitely sensitive mound between her thighs. Either one, or all of them together, were nearly enough to send her over the edge. She grasped handfuls of his hair in her fists and pressed her mouth to his head to keep the whimpering cries of ecstasy locked behind her lips.

They strained together there in the brightly lit hallway of the hotel for several moments longer, both of them trembling uncontrollably, their bodies shifting and sliding against each other, their breathing coming fast and harsh, their blood pounding through their veins . . . and then the bell on the elevator pinged, sounding like a cannon shot in the silent hall.

They pulled apart reluctantly, eyes wide and pupils dilated as they stared at each other for one long, wild second. Willow gasped and turned toward the door, hurriedly yanking the bodice of her dress back in place just as the elevator doors slid open and three men in business suits got out.

Steve swore savagely and went down on his haunches, balancing on the balls of his feet as he picked up her purse and the items that had fallen from it when it hit the carpeted floor. A tube of red lipstick, a monogrammed silver compact, a credit card, her rectangular plastic room key . . . he gathered all but the last into one big hand and stuffed them back into the tiny purse. Then, key card in hand, he stood and opened the door to her room. Neither of them dared look at the other, neither of them said a word as the three businessmen from the elevator walked on past them and down the hall.

Willow turned her head, looking up at him as he stood there, as still as a statue, with her purse and the room key looking like a child's toys in his hands. He was breathing as hard as she was, and his eyes were as avid and hungry as she knew hers must be. All games were forgotten now; she was a woman firmly caught in the throes of a fiery, consuming passion.

"Don't ask me," he pleaded hoarsely, reading the question in her eyes before she could utter it.

But she had to. "Are you coming in?" she whispered.

Steve shook his head and, jaw twitching, shoved the key into her purse and put it in her hand. "I can't."

Willow refused to let the hurt and disappointment show. "Fine," she said, giving him the anger of a woman scorned instead. She stepped across the threshold into her room, then turned and gave him a vixen's smile. "It might interest you to know that I'm not wearing any underwear," she lied, and slammed the door in his face.

Steve groaned and only just managed to keep from pounding his head against the wall.

Willow threw her purse at the closed door with a vicious oath, then sank down on the edge of the bed and dissolved into confused tears.

THE PERSISTENT RINGING of the telephone finally penetrated through the thick veil of dreams that enveloped her, dragging Willow from the arms of a deep, uneasy sleep. She mumbled a protest into her pillow and reached out with one hand, blindly groping for the handset, knocking it off the nightstand in her uncoordinated effort to silence the annoying sound. Rolling onto her side, she grasped the coiled cord, drew it up over the edge of the bed, fumbled for the receiver, and pressed it to her ear.

"What?" she grumbled into the transmitter, groggy and disoriented from a night spent drifting in and out of the most sexually explicit dreams she'd ever experienced.

"It's nearly ten past eight," the subject of those dreams growled in her ear. "You were supposed to meet me in the lobby at eight o'clock sharp."

Willow felt her whole body flush with embarrassment at the sound of his voice, every scandalously salacious detail of those heated nighttime fantasies flickering through her mind in Technicolor clarity. Two bodies, intimately entwined and gleaming with sweat. Two pairs of hands, touching and stroking. Two pairs of lips . . . Fitting retribution for the scandalously salacious way she'd acted last night.

Willow groaned and pulled the pillow over her face, as if he could see her through the telephone.

"Are you still in bed?" he asked suspiciously.

She sat up abruptly, kicking the blankets off, and put her feet on the floor. "No," she said, and stood up to give some credence to her words. "I'm up. I was, ah...I was just about to get into the shower when I heard the phone ring."

"You haven't showered yet? Damn it, Willow." He sounded as grumpy and out of sorts as she felt. "We're supposed to be at Ethan Roberts' at nine. I thought you wanted to get this matter cleared up as quickly as possible." He sighed, loudly, a put-upon male putting up with the exasperating, irritating vagaries of a female. "How long will you be?"

"Fifteen minutes. Twenty, at most," Willow said and hung up without waiting for his reply.

STEVE STOOD DOWNSTAIRS in the lobby, the white house phone clutched in his hand, and wondered what she'd been wearing when she picked up the phone in her room. A silky robe, as soft and smooth as her skin? A hotel towel? Nothing?

The raging demon of unfulfilled desire he thought he'd beaten down during his early-morning workout with the punching bag came back full force. He'd never wanted a woman the way he wanted Willow Ryan, and the teasing game they'd been playing was only part of it. A small part of it, actually. The need in him had been building since the very first time she'd looked up at him with those big golden brown eyes of hers, well *before* she deliberately set out to drive him crazy.

Which was why he had to be so damn careful. He knew he had a weakness for damsels in distress and they, it seemed, had a weakness for him. It was almost on the level of an occupational hazard and the main reason he'd made his rule about not getting sexually involved with his clients. Obviously, he hadn't explained it to her properly yesterday, otherwise she wouldn't have gotten so mad and proceeded to twist his libido into knots. His rule was really more for his clients' protection than his; his amorous urges toward the women he was hired to help were usually mild and easy to resist. And *gone*, once he'd solved their problems for them and they were no longer in distress.

But last night...hell, last night it had felt as if his guts were being yanked out through his navel when he told her no and let her go into that hotel room alone. And the feeling hadn't abated one measly iota since then.

The only consolation was that he knew she'd felt the same way. He'd seen the desire burning behind the anger in her big golden brown eyes, heard the hurt feelings hiding under the taunting words before she slammed the door in his face. He'd heard the muffled thud when her purse hit the hotel room door, too.

Knowing she was as furious, as mad with thwarted desire as he was, somehow made it easier for him to gather up the shattered remnants of his self-control and walk away instead of pounding down the door and demanding to be let in so they could finish what they'd started. In some strange convoluted way, knowing she wanted him with an intensity equal to his desire for her made it easier to wait until the time was right.

If the feelings lasted beyond the end of the case—and he somehow knew they would because feelings like the ones churning up his gut didn't just disappear—then he'd give in to them. And her. But not until then.

"I just hope to hell Ethan Roberts turns out to be her father and we can close this case *today*," he muttered to himself as he returned the handset to its cradle.

The minute she was no longer his client was the same minute she was going to find herself flat on her back in his bed. And she'd be damned lucky if she wasn't bow-legged before he let her up again.

WILLOW GOT HERSELF together in less than twenty minutes, racing through her morning ablutions and a quick application of makeup without her usual meticulous attention to detail. She dressed a bit more carefully, choosing a midcalf apricot-and-ivory-print silk dress with a modest V neck, sensible beige T-strap shoes with small Louis heels and a boxy ivory linen jacket. With her usual small gold hoop earrings and serpentine necklace, she looked cool, composed and professional. In short, like herself and not the wanton temptress of last night.

She wished she could just wipe that whole embarrassing episode out of her mind—and his. It wasn't anything like her normal sensible self. She'd never deliberately teased a man before in her life, no matter how great the provocation, or how mad he'd made her with his arrogant assumptions. "*I'm not wearing any underwear.*" What on earth had she been thinking to say something like that? And, good God, what if he'd given in to her teasing and said yes when she asked him— *begged* him—to come into her room last night?

She'd have awakened this morning in bed with a man she hardly knew!

An arrogant me-Tarzan-you-Jane kind of man, with arms like a stevedore and the dimpled grin of a naughty boy...a man with hard, callused hands, who'd touched her with delicacy and finesse . . . a man who talked like a street tough and acted like a knight in shining armor . . . a man who was all man and made her feel totally, helplessly female in return.

It would have been *glorious*.

And stupid.

And she wasn't going to waste one more second of her time thinking about it.

From now on it was going to be strictly business between them, she promised herself as she hurried down the hall to the elevator. She'd hired him to help her find her father and that was *all* she'd hired him for. The fact that he made her tingle all the way to her toes had nothing to do with anything.

STEVE STOOD WITH HIS ARMS crossed, his shoulder propped against one of the marble pillars in the lobby, watching from his position of stationary surveillance as hotel guests exited and entered through the electronic doors of the hotel's six elevators. He didn't move as Willow stepped out of one exactly seventeen minutes after she'd hung up on him, choosing instead to take the opportunity to observe her—and her mood.

The teasing vamp of last night was gone. She looked cool and fresh this morning, ready for business in a loose, figure-concealing jacket and a long floaty dress with a row of tiny buttons down the front that made his fingers itch to undo them.

If she was still angry about last night it didn't show. She looked nervous, instead, standing in front of the bank of elevators with her bottom lip between her teeth and a tiny frown marring her smooth brow as she searched for him among the potted palms and statuary that decorated the busy hotel lobby. He wondered if her nervousness had to do with embarrassment over what had happened between them last night, or if it sprang from the knowledge that the man they were meeting that morning might turn out to be her father. Either possibility seemed as likely as the other but it would be easier to soothe and reassure her if he knew which it was. He shifted his position slightly, deliberately drawing her attention as her gaze started to wander past him for a third time, hoping he would get a clue from the expression on her face when she saw him.

Her face lit up in that first split second of recognition, like a child's at Christmas, and Steve felt something inside him twist with savage intensity. The feeling was centered higher than his gut, higher than that part of his anatomy that hadn't given him any peace since yesterday morning in his office. It felt a whole lot like a vicious sucker punch to the middle of his chest, the kind that had him fighting to stay on his feet.

And then she blushed and looked down, and he had a few seconds to get his balance back before he had to push away from the support of the marble pillar and stand up under his own power.

They split the distance between them and met half-way, stopping two feet apart in the middle of the opulent lobby, as hesitant and unsure as two teenagers at a freshman mixer. It was a unique and unsettling experience for both of them. Willow, who had made it a point to know just how to conduct herself with grace and poise in any situation. Steve, who was never at a loss for words, even if they were often blunt.

"About last night—" they both said at the same time, and then stopped and smiled awkwardly, each of them motioning for the other to speak.

"Ladies first," Steve insisted, falling back on cowardice and tradition, abruptly deciding he could explain the reasoning behind his rule of noninvolvement at some other time.

Willow swallowed and focused on a point past his left shoulder. "I just wanted to apologize for the, um... for the way I behaved last night," she said, telling herself it was the right thing to do. Just because he'd behaved like an arrogant jerk was no reason for her to have done so. "I behaved abominably and embarrassed both of us in the process. I'm sorry."

"I'm not," Steve murmured, wondering if the feeling in his chest would get better or worse if he leaned down and kissed her.

Willow shifted her gaze to his face. "Not what?"

"Sorry," he said, realizing that the ache in his chest was beginning to feel better the longer he looked at her. "I liked the way you behaved." He grinned, feeling ridiculously happy all of a sudden, although he had no idea why. Lust had never made him giddy before. At least, not since he was about seventeen and had just discovered all the wonderful ways in which girls were different from boys. "I'm looking forward to more of the same kind of behavior in the very near future," he said softly, reaching out to smooth her hair behind her ear. "A lot more."

Willow just stared at him with her mouth open.

"Come on," he said, and took her elbow to hustle her out of the hotel. "Roberts is expecting us for breakfast."

7

ETHAN ROBERTS' HOME was located in the quietly af-
fluent Pacific Palisades area north of Wilshire Boulevard in the section known as the Westside of Los
Angeles. Unlike the more opulent neighborhoods in
Beverly Hills where affluence was proudly flaunted, the
residents of Pacific Palisades chose to hide their wealth
behind concealing stands of trees and ivy-covered
walls. The Roberts' estate was more sheltered than
most, with a camera-monitored security gate and a
long, curving, uphill driveway that effectively shielded
the residence from the view of casual passersby.

The house itself was large but surprisingly modest,
a low rambling structure of weathered gray wood and
pale brick that looked as if it had been standing for
decades. The landscaping consisted of mature trees and
lush, well-groomed flower beds that hinted at regular
care from a professional gardener. A brick patio extended out from one side of the house, furnished with
terra-cotta tubs of bright geraniums and redwood furniture with sturdy canvas cushions. Beyond that was a
half-size blacktop basketball court. Directly in the front
of the house a regulation flagpole rose from the center
of the small, round, grass-covered plot in the middle of

the circular driveway, the American flag at the top fluttering in the light breeze blowing in off the ocean.

There was a steel gray Lincoln Continental in an open bay of the three-car garage, a blue Ford minivan parked, nose out, in the sweeping circular driveway and a shiny red two-wheeled girl's bicycle lying on its side on the grass beneath the flagpole. A large black-and-white cat lay sunning itself on the brick path leading up to the front door.

Steve pulled his Mustang up behind the minivan and killed the engine. There was no sound except the soft flapping of the flag, rippling in the lazy breeze, and the quiet tap of the corded halyard against the flagpole.

"God bless America," Steve said dryly, slanting a wry glance at Willow.

She slanted a glance right back at him as he got out of the car and came around to open her door. "You don't approve of patriotism?" she asked, taking the hand he held out to her.

"Not as long as it's honest." He shut the car door and took her elbow, turning her toward the brick path that led up to the house. "This doesn't feel honest to me."

Looking around her, Willow had to agree. Everything about the scene was just a bit too perfect, a bit too "Mom and country and apple pie," a bit too "we're really just an average American family despite the exclusive address" to ring quite true. It felt as if they'd stepped into a campaign ad specifically designed to play up Ethan Roberts' virtues as a patriotic, clean-living, family-values kind of candidate.

It would have been a lot more convincing if there'd been some signs that lives were actually being lived in the serenely pristine surroundings. A little girl riding the shiny red bike, a couple of kids playing basketball on the empty court, someone lounging with a book out on the cozy brick patio, a cat that actually moved, Willow thought, as she stepped over the sleeping animal.

"Maybe Mom and the kids are out," she suggested. "Saturday errands. Football practice. Shopping for shoes. Stuff like that."

"Then what's the minivan doing parked in the driveway?" Steve countered. "That's the kind of vehicle a rich suburban housewife runs errands in."

The front door swung open as he spoke and a little girl in a bright yellow denim jumper and pink tennis shoes came barreling out the door and down the wide brick steps, plowing into them before she could check her forward progress. Steve reached out and put his hands on her shoulders to keep her from toppling over.

"'Scuse me," she said, ducking out from beneath his hands to chase after the small golden cocker spaniel that had dashed out the door ahead of her, barking wildly as it headed straight for the cat sleeping on the brick path.

Both Steve and Willow turned to watch, knowing she'd be too late to save the pup from its fate. There was a loud hiss as the cat warned him off, then a surprised yelp and a whimper when he charged in anyway and got his tender nose scratched. The little girl bent over, scooping him up in her arms when he turned tail and came running back for protection.

"Mary Catherine, put that dog down before he gets dirty paw prints all over your clothes," a woman ordered as she came out the open front door. She was wearing a crisp white tennis dress with a pleated skirt, a mint green sweater tied by the sleeves around her shoulders and white leather tennis shoes. The little pink pom-poms on her tennis socks bounced above the cuffs of her shoes. Her smooth skin was lightly tanned and her pale champagne blond hair was pulled back into a low, sleek ponytail tied with a pink-and-green grosgrain bow. She carried a leather gym bag and a tennis racket in one hand, and a set of keys in the other. "I haven't got time to have Alma change you again before we leave."

The child turned around, her arms full of squirming dog, ready to argue her case. Dusty paw prints already marred the front of her jumper and the striped T-shirt under it. "But, Mama, Butterscotch needs—"

"Butterscotch needs to learn to fend for himself," said another voice. A tall, handsome man dressed in a burgundy knit polo shirt and pressed tan chinos appeared on the threshold behind the child's mother.

Willow tried not to stare too obviously. The drooping mustache and the long sideburns were gone, of course, discarded relics of his youth. He was clean-shaven now and his conservatively cut, medium brown hair showed a distinguished touch of gray at the temples. There were fine lines of age and experience around his eyes and mouth that hadn't been there in 1970 and he had a certain understated elegance about him, even in the casual clothes, that hadn't been apparent in the photographs Willow carried in her purse. But he was so indisputably the same man pictured with his arm slung around her mother's shoulders that Willow wondered why she hadn't recognized him before Steve pointed it out to her. She realized it was because she had unconsciously been looking for the boy her father had been, not the man he had become.

It was Ethan Roberts, in the flesh. The man who might—or might not, she reminded herself—be her father.

"Put the dog down, please," he said to the little girl. "And come here and apologize to our guests for nearly knocking them over."

Mary Catherine obeyed immediately. "Yes, Daddy." She put the puppy down, leaving him to his fate, and retraced her steps up the brick path, ineffectively brushing at the dusty paw prints on her clothes as she did so.

"What do you say?" her father asked when she reached the front steps where Willow and Steve were standing.

"I 'pologize for almost knocking you down," the child said earnestly. "I shouldn't have been running. But Butterscotch isn't s'posed to be loose in the front yard."

She watched her father out of the corner of her eye as she spoke, as if to make sure of his approval. When he nodded, the tension in the child's face faded into relief. She turned and bolted for the minivan.

"Walk," he hollered after her, then shrugged and shook his head at his guests. "My daughter, Mary Catherine," he said, by way of introduction. "And my wife—" he put his arm around the woman's shoulders as she came down the steps and gave her a quick squeeze "—Joanna."

"Lovely to meet you," Joanna Roberts said pleasantly, nodding at each of them in lieu of shaking hands. "I really hate to greet and run but I'm already late. I have to drop Mary Catherine off at her play group before I go to the club," she explained. "We'll be back by three," she said to her husband, tilting her cheek for a kiss that just managed to miss connecting. "Make sure Alma puts the dog back in his run, won't you?"

As she headed down the brick path to the van, Steve wondered if anyone else realized that Ethan Roberts hadn't actually introduced them to his wife by name. Was that a deliberate omission, he wondered, or just an oversight? And was the fact that Roberts' wife and child were leaving just as Steve and Willow arrived mere coincidence or the result of a watchful eye on the camera that monitored the front gate?

A man who was prepared to answer a few casual questions about a woman he had dated twenty-five years ago would have nothing to hide from his family; a man who thought he was about to be confronted by the daughter he had abandoned before her birth probably wouldn't want his wife to witness the confrontation.

"I'm assuming you are Ms. Ryan," Ethan said pleasantly, turning to look at Willow as his wife and daughter drove away.

"Yes." She nodded. "I'm Willow Ryan. And this is my—" how did one introduce a private investigator? "—associate, Steve Hart," she said.

The two men shook hands. Rather warily, Willow thought, as if they were using the brief clasp of hands to test each other's mettle.

"Let's go inside, then, shall we?" Ethan stepped back, motioning them up the wide brick steps and through the door ahead of him with a gracious sweep of his arm.

The inside of the house was like the outside, quietly luxurious and meticulously maintained with a folksy, all-American charm that felt too studied to be quite real, like some novice set designer's idea of what a politician's home should look like. The color scheme consisted of a subdued mix of navy-and-cream prints and plaids, with the judicious use of red as an accent. The furniture was mostly Early American with a few English antiques thrown in. The tall mirror in the foyer had an eagle carved into its gilded frame. A large family portrait, painted in oils, hung over the fireplace in the spacious living room.

In it, Joanna Roberts sat in a gold brocade wing chair, with a younger version of Mary Catherine sitting in her lap. A boy who appeared to be about eleven or twelve years old sat perched on the arm of her chair. Another boy, perhaps fifteen or so, stood by her side. Ethan Roberts stood behind them all, one hand on the back of his wife's chair, one hand on the shoulder of the standing boy, proud patriarch of the perfect all-American family.

"We had that painted a few years ago," Ethan said, noticing that Willow was staring at the portrait, "when the boys were home from the academy during Christmas vacation. That's Edward," he told her, gesturing toward the boy sitting on the arm of the chair. "And my oldest son, Peter. And, of course, you recognize Mary Catherine. She was about three when that was done."

"You have a lovely family," Willow said, wondering if they might be her family, too. A sweet little sister...brothers... She felt Steve's hand settle gently on the small of her back and took a quick breath, tamping down the trembling emotions the thought of a real family evoked. It was too soon to be thinking of them as family.

"You must be very proud of them," she said easily, steadied by the warm hand on her back.

"Yes, I am," Ethan agreed. "Very proud." He turned his head, glancing down the hall to his right. "Alma!" he called impatiently.

A middle-aged Hispanic woman in a classic maid's uniform answered his summons.

"Mary Catherine's dog is in the front yard again," he said, speaking to the maid as if it were somehow her fault. "See that he gets put back in his run. And put her bike back in the garage where it belongs."

The maid nodded.

"I'll expect breakfast out on the deck in—" he glanced at the heavy gold Rolex on his wrist "—fifteen minutes."

The maid nodded again and went outside to fetch the dog and put the child's bicycle away.

Ethan Roberts turned a charming smile on his guests. "This way," he said, motioning them through the living room, toward the wide, multipaned glass doors that stood open to a cantilevered redwood deck with a spectacular view of the distant Pacific.

BY MUTUAL, IF SILENT, agreement the three of them kept the conversation light and inconsequential as Alma quietly and efficiently served an al fresco breakfast of individual fresh fruit salads in chilled bowls and spicy *huevos rancheros*.

"You can leave the pot on the table," Ethan said to her as she filled his coffee cup for the second time. "I'll call you if we need anything else."

Without a word, the maid set the coffeepot down on the glass-topped patio table and turned to go.

"Muchas gracias, señora," Steve said, thanking her for the breakfast. *"El desayuno estuvo delicioso."*

The maid looked up, as if startled to be addressed politely and in her own language, and then smiled shyly. *"De nada, señor,"* she murmured softly, and pulled the glass doors closed, leaving the three of them alone on the deck.

"You speak Spanish," Willow said admiringly.

Steve shrugged. "It comes in handy in my line of work."

"And what exactly is your line of work?" Ethan Roberts asked. "I don't think anyone has actually said."

"I'm a private investigator," Steve said, watching to see how the other man took the news.

"I see," Ethan said, his eyes lowered as he lifted his coffee cup to his lips. He took a small sip, then put the coffee cup down and looked directly at Willow. "The message I got via my campaign manager said you have some questions you think I might be able to answer about your mother."

"Yes, I . . ." Willow didn't quite know how to put the question to him now that she had the chance. It wasn't an easy thing to ask. "I was wondering, ah...that is..." She took a quick breath and began again. "I guess I should begin by telling you that my mother died when I was five months old," she said, looking at him closely to see how he reacted to the news.

"I'm sorry to hear that," Ethan murmured sympathetically. "I had no idea. When Donna dropped out of sight all those years ago, I guess I assumed that she'd just—" he made a brushing-away motion with one hand "—quit the business."

"Yes, well . . . I know very little about her and nothing at all about the man who was, or is, my father. I've been trying to reconstruct her life here in Los Angeles before I was born. I know you worked together on television and that you lived in the same apartment building and I . . ."

"And you're wondering if I can tell you anything about her?"

"Yes." Willow seized on that as a good place to start. "Yes, I was wondering if you could tell me anything about her. Anything at all that you might remember."

"I remember her quite well, actually," he said. "She was a stunning young woman. Really quite spectacular looking." He smiled across the table at Willow. "You resemble her a great deal."

Willow smiled back but made no comment. She resembled her mother slightly, around the eyes, but no more than that. To have Ethan Roberts say otherwise smacked of an insincerity that made her uncomfortable in some indefinable way, as if he were flattering her for a purpose.

"How *well* did you know Donna Ryan?" Steve asked bluntly, impatient with all the fancy tap dancing around the subject. He knew Willow was trying to handle the whole thing as diplomatically as possible, tactfully working her way toward the real question, hoping Roberts would bring it up himself and save her from having to ask it. But Steve had the deep-down gut feeling that if they waited for Roberts to bring it up, they'd wait forever. The man had the natural caginess of a born politician, unwilling to be the first to broach a potentially unpleasant subject.

"Did you date her?" Steve prodded, wanting to see how the other man would reply to a question they already knew the answer to.

"Date her?" Ethan said, as if there were some doubt as to what the word meant. He shrugged. "I guess you could say I dated her."

"You guess?" Steve didn't even try to keep the sarcasm out of his voice.

Willow shot him a look across the table, silently censuring him for his bluntness, but he ignored her.

"Either you dated her or you didn't," he said. "Which is it?"

"The studio arranged for us to go out two or three times. Publicity," Ethan said, and paused to sip from his coffee cup again. "Studios still did things like that back then and actors went along with it. Especially young actors just starting out in the business. Your mother—" he smiled at Willow as he set his cup back down "—was, as I said, a stunning young woman. The studio heads thought it would be good for both our careers and the show if we appeared to have a personal relationship. It was business."

"According to the manager at the Bachelor Arms, you were the one who told her about the vacancy in the building," Steve said. "Was that business, too?"

"I knew she was looking for an apartment. One was available in my building. It was as simple as that."

"Jack Shannon remembers it a little differently," Steve said, watching the other man carefully, hoping for a reaction to the name.

"Jack Shannon?" The flare of surprise in his eyes was quickly hidden behind a pleasant smile. "Now that's a name I haven't heard in a while, although I have seen his by line in the *Times* of late. How is ol' Jack?"

Steve ignored the question. "Ol' Jack said you used to brag about going out with Donna Ryan. That you made sure everyone in the building knew about it."

Ethan's smile died. "It's quite possible that I did," he said, his gaze gone cold and steely as it met Steve's across the table. "I was a young man, unattached at the time. She was a beautiful young woman. I may have cherished certain—" he glanced at Willow as if to apologize for what he was about to say "—lustful thoughts in that direction. They were completely unreciprocated, I assure you."

"Then you didn't sleep with her?"

"Sleep with her?" Ethan Roberts managed to look outraged, insulted and innocent, all at the same time. "No. Definitely not. I don't know why you'd even suggest such a thing," he said to Steve, "especially in the presence of her daughter."

"Because we thought that, maybe, I might be *your* daughter, too," Willow said.

"*My* daughter?" Ethan Roberts looked at her as if she'd lost her mind. "No, I . . ." His eyes hardened. "If this is some sort of blackmail scheme, you can forget it." He pushed back from the table and stood, righteous indignation and outrage in every line of his body. "Get out of my house before I call the police," he ordered them. "Now."

Steve reached over and put his hand on Willow's arm, stopping her from rising from her chair. "Take it easy, Roberts," he said, his voice deliberately lazy. He knew a bluff when he heard one, and the threat to call the police had been just that. A bluff. "This isn't a shakedown. My client isn't after money or publicity. If she was, she'd have already gone to the papers with this. All she wants to know is if there's any possibility you might be her father. Any possibility at all."

"I told you. No. No possibility at all. None whatsoever."

"All right." Steve nodded agreeably. "You're not her father." He waited a beat. "Do you know who might be?"

"How would I know something like that?"

"You worked on the same television show. Lived in the same building. Shared some of the same friends. It's conceivable you might have known who she was involved with back then." He glanced over at Willow. "Show him the pictures," he said to her.

Willow reached down and picked up the slim beige leather shoulder bag she had wedged between her hip and the arm of her chair. Opening it, she pulled out the five pictures taken of her mother and her friends at the Bachelor Arms and handed them to Ethan Roberts.

"And the card," Steve said.

Willow handed that over, too.

"Neither you nor Zeke Blackstone has changed beyond recognition in twenty-five years," Steve said, watching Ethan's face as he sat back down and began to thumb through the photographs. "And the Bachelor Arms was easy to identify, especially since I drive by it a couple of times a week. Once we had that, it was easy to find out the names of the other two guys in the pictures. The manager at the BA said he was pretty sure both you and Eric Shannon had dated Donna but he didn't know how serious it was in either case." He paused, waiting and watching while Ethan opened and read the greeting card. "I take it you didn't send that to her?" he said when Ethan laid the card down on the table.

"No." Ethan shook his head. "I didn't." He looked back down at the photographs, shifting them around on the table with the tip of one finger. "Maybe Eric did."

"Maybe." Steve shrugged. "But with him being dead and unavailable for comment it would be kind of hard to prove either way," he said, so callously that Willow's eyes widened in surprise.

Steve gave her a small admonishing shake of his head that kept her quiet.

"The manager gave us quite an earful," he went on easily, probing for a reaction. Any reaction. "All the gory details about the night Eric Shannon committed suicide, along with some cock-and-bull story about a ghost in a cursed mirror."

"I'd forgotten about the mirror," Ethan murmured, still looking at the pictures.

"Amberson claimed you'd seen something in it, too."

Ethan looked up then. "Amberson's got a screw loose," he said flatly, a hint of anger in his tone.

"No question about that," Steve agreed, wondering at the vehemence of the other man's response. Aside from his outburst when he accused them of blackmail, it was the strongest reaction they'd gotten from him. "Jack Shannon said pretty much the same thing about him. He also said he and his wife both saw something in the mirror themselves," Steve added, trying to find out if the reaction had been in response to Amberson or the ridiculous story about the mirror.

"Faith Shannon said it changed their lives," Willow added, immediately sensing what Steve was up to and trying to add fuel to the fire.

But Ethan Roberts wasn't giving them any more. "I always thought Jack went a little crazy after his brother died," he said, his politician's mask hiding every emotion except a kind of wry amusement. He gathered up the pictures and the card, and handed them back to Willow. "I'm sorry," he said. "I can't tell you any more than you already seem to know."

Steve shrugged, as if he'd expected that answer, and rose to his feet. "We knew it was a long shot," he said, stepping behind Willow's chair to pull it out for her. "A handful of pictures and a greeting card signed with the initial *E* aren't a whole hell of a lot to go on. Twenty-five years make for a long, cold trail. I told Willow that when she hired me."

"I'm not giving up hope just yet," Willow said, taking a moment to tuck the card and pictures back into her purse before she, too, rose to her feet. "There's still that box of stuff Mr. Amberson gave Jack from apartment 1-G. There might be a letter or pictures or maybe even a journal of some sort in there. Jack did say his brother was a writer, remember," she said brightly, smiling up at Steve like the birdbrained bimbo he knew she wasn't. "And we haven't talked to Zeke Blackstone yet. He might know something that will help." She settled the strap of her purse over her right shoulder and held out her hand. "Thank you for your time, and for breakfast, Mr. Roberts," she said briskly. "I'm sorry if we inconvenienced or upset you in any way."

"Not at all," Ethan said smoothly. "I'm only sorry I couldn't be of more help to you myself." He escorted them to the glass doors that opened onto the deck, stepping into the house ahead of them to tug on the embroidered bellpull that hung just inside the door. "Alma will see you out," he said, as the maid appeared in answer to his summons. "I have some calls to make."

They followed the silent maid through the living room and across the foyer to the front door where Steve paused, turning to speak to her in soft, sibilant Spanish.

The maid looked over her shoulder, toward the hallway where Ethan Roberts had disappeared, then turned back and answered Steve's question with a rapid flow of words.

"*Gracias, señora.*" Steve reached into his pocket and took out a business card, holding it out to her with another incomprehensible flow of Spanish.

She hesitated for a moment, then snatched it out of his hand, speaking quietly as she slipped it—and the twenty-dollar bill he offered with it—into the pocket of her uniform.

"What was that all about?" Willow asked, as they walked down the brick pathway to the car. "What did you say to her?"

"I asked her how long she'd been with the family."

"And?" she said, giving him an impatient glance as he handed her into the passenger seat.

"Almost eight years." He shut the car door and went around to the driver's side, making her wait for the rest of it.

"What else?" she demanded, turning to face him as he slid behind the wheel. "I know she said more than that."

"Are you sure you want to know? It doesn't cast your potential papa in a very pretty light."

She gave him a level look from under her brows. "I told you I'm not some fragile flower," she reminded him. "I want the truth. That's what I hired you for."

"It seems Roberts' perfect little family isn't quite so perfect as it appears on the outside."

Willow gave a small snort of disgust, letting him know she didn't need someone else to tell her that.

Steve grinned. "You picked up on that, too, huh?"

"It didn't take a bloodhound," she said dryly. "Or a high-priced P.I. A myopic poodle could have figured out that everything isn't what it appears to be around here." She shook her head. "Nothing's as perfect as all this appears to be."

Steve's grin grew wider. "Damn, I like your style, sweetheart," he said, giving it the old Bogie imitation. "Why don't you quit the accounting business and part-

ner up with me? We made a damn good team in there."
He cocked his head toward the house, silently indicating the way they'd instinctively played off each other in their questioning of Roberts. "I could turn you into an ace operative in no time."

"Thanks," she said, pleased by his playful words of praise, "but I like the accounting business. And you're stalling. Answer my question. What else did Alma have to say?"

"Well—" he put the car in gear and headed it down the winding driveway "—it seems that Alma Rodriguez was hired a few months after Roberts and his new wife got custody of his two boys. Joanna was pregnant with little Mary Catherine and, apparently, the boys were too much for her to handle, especially with the campaign, and all. Roberts ran for a seat in the California House of Representatives in '88," Steve told her. "Señora Rodriguez says the boys acted like they hated their father, and he didn't seem to care much for them, either. After the election was over, he shipped them off to a military academy on the East Coast. Apparently, he trots them out when the occasion calls for a show of family unity."

"Then it's more than just extra window dressing for the public, isn't it? The whole thing is just one big lie. The house. The happy family. Everything." She was quiet for a minute, turning it around in her mind. "Which probably means that he was lying about my mother, too. Lying about his relationship with her. And about me."

"We could call a halt to this right now," Steve said. "Just stop digging and let it drop."

"No." Willow shook her head. "I've wondered about it for too many years already, telling myself that knowing wouldn't make any difference to my life, but wanting to know anyway. Needing to know." She shrugged. "Maybe knowing won't make any difference to how I feel about myself. Maybe it will make me feel better. Or worse. But good or bad, I *have* to know." She ran her hands down her thighs, smoothing nonexistent wrinkles out of her skirt. "I want you to keep digging until you find out the truth."

8

"SO," WILLOW SAID as they finally exited Ethan Roberts' upscale neighborhood and merged into the eastbound traffic on San Vincente Boulevard. "What's our next step?"

Steve slanted her a glance out of the corner of his eye. "*Our* next step?"

"You did say we should be partners."

"I was speaking facetiously."

"What?" She turned in the seat, crossing her legs as she angled her body to face him. "You mean you were just leading me on?"

"Don't start," he warned.

Willow felt herself blush. "Sorry," she said, quickly shifting around to face the windshield again. "I wasn't thinking."

"Look, I didn't mean... Oh, hell, don't be mad. I was just teasing you."

"I'm not mad," Willow said. "I'm embarrassed."

"Embarrassed? What the hell for?"

"We went down this road last night, remember? I made a huge fool of myself in front of you once already. I'm not looking to do it again."

"Gee, that's too bad," he said, giving her a teasing, sidelong look out of the corner of his eye. "I was looking forward to a repeat performance."

"There isn't going to be any repeat performance," Willow mumbled.

"Oh, yes, there is," he assured her. "You can count on it."

There was such certainty in his voice, such absolute male arrogance in his tone, that Willow turned her head to look at him, her embarrassment all but forgotten. "God, you really think you're irresistible, don't you?"

"To you, I am."

Willow opened her mouth to refute his statement, then closed it when no words came out. There were no words to refute the truth.

"If it's any comfort, it works both ways," he said. "All I've been able to think about for the last twenty-six hours and—" he glanced at the clock on the dashboard "—eighteen minutes is getting between your legs."

Willow squeaked like a frightened Victorian virgin and instinctively clamped her knees together.

Steve laughed softly, sexily, the sound brushing over Willow's nerve endings like warm fur over bare skin. "That isn't going to do you any good," he said, and reached over, running the blunt tip of one finger up the seam between her legs by feel alone, from knees to crotch, very lightly, barely skimming along the material of her dress. "See?" he said, when she gasped and drew in a shuddering breath.

She slapped his hand away, a moment after she should have if she'd really meant it.

He returned his hand to the steering wheel, grasping it tightly in order to keep from reaching over and sliding his hand under her skirt to repeat the caress.

She stared at her lap and wondered what would happen if she reached over and did the same thing to him that he'd just done to her.

He shifted in his seat as if she had.

They rode in strained, breathless silence for several long miles, past the tall coral trees that shaded the center median of San Vincente Boulevard, and the huge red barn of a building that housed the Brentwood Country Mart, both of them trying to think of something to say that couldn't be construed as a sexual come-on. Both of them failed miserably because the only words that came to mind were ones that had to do with the wild feeling ricocheting back and forth between them.

"I'm not going to say I'm sorry about this," Steve said, finally, staring straight out the windshield as he turned from San Vincente onto Wilshire, "because I'm not. Except for the timing, that is. The timing stinks. But as for the rest of it, well..." He shrugged, his broad shoulders moving uneasily under the material of his navy sport jacket. "I'm a man, you're a woman, and it is what it is," he said, not quite ready to put a name to exactly what that was. "We're just going to have to work around it for now."

"Work around it how?" Willow wondered out loud.

He dared a glance at her. "Were you serious about that offer to set up an accounting system for me?"

"Sure." Willow nodded. "I'm always serious about money."

"Then how about if I drop you off at my office so you can get started on it?"

"While you do what?"

"Routine stuff," he said. "I've got a few new questions for my buddy down at the LAPD. Then I want to talk to a couple of people I know who are plugged into the political scene in this town. Maybe stop by the morgue at the *Times* and catch up on my reading if there's time."

"I could help you with that."

Steve shook his head. "I'll get it done a lot faster without you, believe me. And not just because you won't be there to drive me crazy," he told her, "but because I know what to look for. You don't."

Though she wanted to, Willow couldn't really argue with that. "Okay. Take me back to your office. I'll get started on that mess you call an accounting system."

STEVE HAD CLEANED UP his office since yesterday morning and the computer and its various components had been unwrapped and were sitting, brand-new and untouched, on top of the desk next to the green account ledger and an accordion-pleated cardboard file jammed untidily full of invoices, receipts and various miscellaneous bits of paper.

As Willow took off her ivory jacket, hanging it on the back of one of the chairs in front of the desk, she noticed a large framed photograph sitting next to the telephone on the credenza. Intrigued by this unexpected glimpse into his private life, she circled the desk and picked it up for a closer look.

The picture had been taken on a boat, with blue sky and a smooth white sail in the background. An older man and woman, presumably Steve's parents, stood side by side with their hands on the spoked wooden wheel. Steve stood behind his mother, a little to one side, with his cheek pressed to hers and her hand lifted, resting against the side of his face to hold him there. A young woman, somewhere in her mid-twenties and with a grin just enough like Steve's for Willow to safely assume she was his sister, had struck a similar pose next to their father. The older man's hand was raised, holding his daughter's blowing hair out of his face and obscuring his mouth, but Willow could tell, just by the twinkle in his eyes that was so like Steve's, that he was smiling. Steve's strong arms encompassed them all, one hand curved around his mother's biceps, the other reaching around behind them all to rest on top of his sister's hand where it lay on their father's shoulder. The pose looked completely unstudied, as if they had stopped whatever they'd been doing to mug for the camera. The very naturalness and the easy affection they all so obviously had for each other took Willow aback for a second.

Her image of Steve Hart hadn't included a loving, affectionate family. Somehow, she'd formed the impression that he was a loner. Maybe it was his obvious air of independence, the sense of utter self-sufficiency he seemed to exude. Maybe it was just the fact that he was a private investigator that had given her the idea; the public imagination usually cast men—and women—of his profession as mavericks. Obviously, she was wrong. She put the picture down, giving it one last lingering look, and went to work on the computer.

It took her less than thirty minutes to connect all the components and get them running. It took another fifteen to load the accounting software. How long it would take to make sense of his personal accounting system was another matter entirely. She stood up and stretched, telling herself she'd get busy on it in a minute or two, and started on a slow tour of the office.

She began by taking a few experimental jabs at the punching bag hanging in the corner, curling her hand into a loose fist and striking at the smudged spots that showed where he habitually landed his blows. The surface was harder than she expected it to be, the bag not nearly as easy to move as she'd imaged. She put both hands against it and shoved. It moved a few inches at most before settling back into place.

"Jeez," she muttered to herself, her tone admiring. "No wonder he has shoulders like Rocky Balboa."

She inspected the coffeepot and the small store of supplies he kept to go with it—a can of ground coffee, paper filters, two plain ceramic mugs, both spanking clean, a small jar of powdered creamer and individual packets of real sugar—all neatly stacked in a large rectangular plastic box on top of one of the files.

And then, finally, after telling herself she absolutely wouldn't, she started poking into unlocked desk drawers and snooping in his files. He had, after all, she rationalized, given her complete access to his financial records. And what could be more personal than that?

But Steve Hart was a careful man. The only unlocked file drawer held folded towels and clean clothes—gym shorts, T-shirts, thick white socks and a spandex jockstrap she spent a few heated minutes imagining him wearing. There was nothing incriminating in any of the desk drawers. No photographs of old girlfriends. No notes from rejected, love-starved clients. She found pens and pencils, paper clips, boxes of staples and rubber bands, quality white bond stationery with his name in black ink across the top and small three-by-five-inch notebooks all neatly stacked. All of which convinced her that the mess she'd seen— was it only yesterday morning?—had been some temporary aberration on his part, probably brought on by trying to make sense of his own accounting system. Contrary to his offhand remark about not being much of a housekeeper, the man was obviously as neat as the proverbial pin, as well as careful of his clients' privacy.

She was just about to give up her haphazard search for clues into his life and personality and get back to work when she found his cache of condoms in the lower right-hand drawer.

She felt a rushing tide of heat spread through her body, starting with her face and working downward over the suddenly aching tips of her breasts, curling through her belly to lie coiled and hungry, between her legs.

She slammed the drawer shut and pressed both hands to her face, as if she could somehow hold back the emotions that flooded through her, and then reached down and opened the drawer again, cautiously, like a child irresistibly drawn to touch a tempting, forbidden treasure that she knew ahead of time was only going to get her into trouble.

There were three boxes of thirty-six condoms each, assorted colors and textures, reservoir-tipped, size extra large. One box was open, the top neatly torn off to allow easy access to the contents. It was half-empty.

Back on the commune when she was growing up, her aunt Sharon had seen to it that each and every kid on the place got all the information he or she would ever need about sexual responsibility and the various methods of birth control, starting with a straightforward, no-nonsense talk about human reproduction the first time any one of them asked where babies came from.

Carefully, with the tips of two fingers, Willow reached into the open box and pulled out one of the individually wrapped foil packets, automatically putting one of those lessons to good use. The packet was soft and supple in her fingers, indicating that it hadn't been sitting in the desk drawer for any great length of time.

Not only was Steve Hart neat, careful, conscientious and a loving son and brother, he was also, judging by the evidence in her hands, a very busy boy when it came to the ladies.

Willow wondered if that fact made her feel better or worse about the overwhelming attraction she felt for him. On the one hand, she didn't like the idea of being one of a crowd. On the other, there was undoubtedly a great deal to be said for a man who knew what he was doing in bed. And she had no doubt—none at all—that Steve Hart knew exactly what he was doing. In bed or out.

The question was, did she?

This insane attraction she felt toward him was something entirely outside of her experience. Oh, she'd had lovers. Two, to be exact. But the feelings they had evoked in her—even in the throes of what she'd obviously mistakenly thought was passion!—were lukewarm compared to what Steve Hart made her feel just by looking at her with that teasing sideways glance of his.

She had no idea where they were headed with this—except, it seemed, to bed—but she wanted to follow it to the end. The lure was as irresistible as it was unfathomable.

With a soft heartfelt sigh, Willow dropped the foil packet back in the box and closed the drawer, determined to buckle down and make some sense of his ledger. Immersing herself in debits and credits, income and outgo, profits and losses was the best way she knew to get her mind off of anything that was bothering her.

WILLOW SURFACED nearly five hours later, having made a half-dozen neat stacks of invoices and receipts, placing them according to her best guess as to what they were for. Steve seemed to use a basic, and vastly inadequate, single-entry accounting system. Income in one column, expenses in another, with no provisions at all for dividing anything out into any of the business categories the Internal Revenue Service would find acceptable should they ever decide to audit him.

Most of the invoices and receipts were fairly easy to categorize once she separated them out—office supplies and equipment, auto expenses, professional fees, taxes and the like. But there were dozens of slips of paper, torn from small lined notepads like the ones he had stacked in his desk drawer, marked with, at best, a name, a date and an amount. She suspected that, like the money he had tried to give Ken Amberson yesterday and the twenty dollars he had given Ethan Roberts' maid this morning, they were bribes for information.

There was nothing in any of the vast mountain of IRS material she had ever read that covered bribes as a deductible business expense.

In the end, she gave it up, relegating them to the pile marked Miscellaneous.

Then, having done all she could until she talked to Steve, she neatly relabeled each section of the cardboard file in accordance with the newly established categories, slipped the invoices and receipts into them, and closed the entire package with two wide blue rubber bands.

Placing a Post-it note on the top that said Do Not Touch! in case Steve came back to the office while she was gone, she slung the strap of her purse crosswise over her torso, closed up the office, and headed across the street to the Greek deli for a quick sugar fix and a cup of coffee.

BY FIVE-THIRTY, Steve had dug up more than he wanted to know about the life and character of Ethan Roberts. By all accounts from people who were in a position to know, the man was a coldhearted, calculating bastard who wasn't above using anybody he had to in order to get what he wanted. Including his own children.

Steve had no trouble at all believing he could have casually impregnated Willow's mother, then abandoned her and their unborn child to whatever fate had in store for them. It wouldn't have been the last time he'd done it, nor, most likely, the first.

The only trouble was, there was no way to prove it, short of a blood test, and Steve had no illusions about the possibility of getting Ethan Roberts to voluntarily agree to something like that. Willow could take it to the newspapers, of course, or threaten to—assuming she was willing to take that route to try to force Roberts to admit to his paternity. But Steve doubted it would work.

Politics, power and the electorate being what they were, Roberts could probably manage to sidestep any scandal her accusations might bring on his way to the Senate by simply denying them. Hell, Washington was full of men who'd managed to get themselves elected in spite of their unsavory private lives.

And maybe, if she was lucky, Ethan Roberts wasn't her father.

In which case, they probably *still* couldn't get him to take a blood test, because agreeing to do so would be looked at as an admission of the possibility that he might be her father.

No, any way you looked at it, Ethan Roberts' wisest course was continued denial, no matter what Willow did or said. That way, no one would ever know for sure. They might suspect and whisper, but no one would ever know for sure.

Including Willow.

Steve hated to think what that would do to her. After screwing up the courage to start looking after twenty-four years of wondering about it, to hit a dead end now would be a crushing blow. No, not crushing, he decided, instantly changing his mind. Even on the basis of two days' acquaintance, he knew Willow Ryan was too strong and too smart to let a thing like this crush her. But it would be a blow. It would hurt.

And he hated to think of her hurting.

He flexed his hands against the steering wheel, thinking with distinct pleasure of beating the truth out of Ethan Roberts. He imagined smashing his fist into that aristocratic nose, landing a couple of solid jabs in that pampered midsection, meting out some tiny measure of punishment for all the pain Roberts had caused to the vulnerable women and children who had been sacrificed to his career.

Of course, he thought with a grin, Willow probably wouldn't think it was such a good idea. Woman tended to prefer a more nonviolent approach to solving problems.

But, hell, maybe he was just borrowing trouble, anyway. Maybe they'd find something in Jack Shannon's box of memories that would prove Eric Shannon was her father. Maybe Zeke—*Ezekiel*, he reminded himself—maybe Ezekiel Blackstone would turn out to be the one. Maybe the operative he'd put on the trail of Donna's old roommate, Christine Loudon, would turn up something. At this point, anything was possible.

That was the tack he would take with Willow, he decided, as he maneuvered his Mustang into an empty parking space just two doors down from his office. He'd play up the positive aspects of the case and ignore the negatives.

And hope like hell they found some answers before a very important and cherished part of his anatomy exploded under the force of constant, unrelieved arousal. He'd always thought anticipation was one of the many delicious pleasures of sex but since meeting Willow he was beginning to change his mind.

The anticipation was killing him.

Even now, he realized, as he climbed out of the Mustang and pocketed his keys, just the simple anticipation of seeing her again had his lips turning up in an idiot's grin and his heart racing uncomfortably fast. His unprecedented reaction to her was something he was going to have to take some time to think about soon, he promised himself.

And then he caught sight of her, coming out of the Greek deli across the street from his office, and he experienced that same savage twist in his chest that had taken him by surprise that morning. And he realized he didn't have to think about it, after all.

It wasn't lust. It was love.

He, Steve Hart, tough-guy private investigator, a man who'd been making love to women for a lot of years, without ever finding one he could love for a lifetime, had fallen head over heels in love at first sight. With a client. And wasn't that a kick in the pants!

"Willow," he hollered, raising his arm to get her attention from across the street.

She looked around at the sound of his voice, her face lighting up with the same happy glow that had caused him to nearly lose his balance that morning in the hotel lobby. She lifted her arm in return, waving back, and started across the street toward him.

"I can't *believe* what a mess your books are in," she shouted, beginning to scold him before she was even halfway across the street. "You should be ashamed of yourself."

Steve just raised his hands, palms up, and smiled.

She laughed out loud and shook her head, watching him as she moved forward, neglecting to check traffic as she crossed the yellow centerline.

She was less than halfway across the lane when Steve caught a flash of something out of the corner of his eye: a dark blue car, moving too fast; a driver in a brimmed hat. He rushed forward, squeezing between two parked cars, shouting at Willow to get out of the way.

She stopped, puzzled by his actions, then turned, seeing the car bearing down on her, and tried desperately to reverse direction and scramble out of the way.

Steve hit her, waist high, in a bruising tackle, bearing her back over the median line. He felt something graze his calf, nearly jerking him around, and then they hit the ground and rolled. There was a screech of tires. Horns honked. Someone screamed. They came to an abrupt stop, thudding up against the rear wheel of a parked car on the other side of the street, with his body curved over hers and his arms tight around her, desperately trying to shelter her from further harm.

It took a second for him to realize he wasn't seriously hurt, and then another to realize she might be.

He loosened his arms a little, very gently, and pulled back so he could see down into her face. "Willow?" he murmured in an agonized whisper. "Willow, sweetheart, are you all right?"

She stirred against him, pushing at his chest to get some air. "Aside from being crushed to death, I think so."

He was too far-gone to appreciate the attempt at humor. "Do you hurt anywhere?" He lifted himself farther away from her as he spoke, levering himself up onto his knees beside her. "Are you bleeding?"

"Good God!" someone said before Willow could answer him. "Are you people all right? Do you need an ambulance?"

"Yes. Call an ambulance," Steve said. "She's hurt."

"No," Willow said, struggling to sit up under his restraining hands. "I'm all right. Really. I don't need an ambulance."

Steve helped her to sit up, gently, lifting her so that she sat with her back to the wheel of the car. "Are you sure you're okay?"

"My elbows sting like the dickens but everything seems to be where it belongs." She lifted her hand and touched the side of his face. "How about you? Are you all right?"

"I'm fine," he said, brushing away her concern, along with the throbbing in his right calf. "Can you stand up?"

She nodded gingerly and they helped each other, holding on to each other's arms as they got to their feet.

"Okay?" Steve asked when they were both upright. He untangled the strap of her purse, gently pulling it down from around her neck. "Everything in working order?"

"Fine," she said. "How about you?"

"I'll live." His heart would never be the same, but he'd definitely live. Keeping one hand on her arm to steady her in case she felt faint, he turned toward the small crowd that had gathered around them.

"Which one of you is the driver of that goddamn car?" he demanded angrily, ready to lay into some-one—anyone!—for the injuries done to Willow.

"It didn't stop, man," said a kid dressed in baggy knee-length shorts and an oversize T-shirt. "Just kept right on goin'."

"Did anyone get the license number?"

"I didn't get no numbers, man. But it was a dark blue Honda Accord. And it sure was comin' fast, like a bat outta hell. Looked like the driver was *tryin'* to hit your lady."

"Are you sure about that?" Steve demanded. His gaze scanned the crowd. "Did anyone else get that impression?"

"It could have been, I guess," said an older woman who was standing on the sidewalk with a bright green shopping bag dangling from the crook of her arm. "It looked like he might have swerved toward you instead of away like someone would normally do."

"He?" Steve said. "The driver was a man?"

The woman hesitated. "Yes," she said. "I think so."

"Naw, it was a woman," the kid said. "She had blond hair and was wearin' a hat. And she was aimin' the car right at you," he added, warming to the story.

"What kind of hat?" Steve asked.

The woman walked away then, along with everyone else except the kid. There was nothing to see. No blood; no guts; nobody maimed or dying.

"Just a hat. Not cool, like mine." He reached up behind him to touch the bill of the baseball cap he wore. "One of them fancy lady hats that sticks out all around."

"You mean with a brim?" Steve made a motion with his hand, sketching a hat brim in the air around his head.

"Yeah," the kid said. "With one of them brims. Pulled kinda low over her face."

"Did you see what color it was?"

He shrugged. "Dark," he said. "Maybe black or brown."

Steve nodded and dug a hand into his pocket. "Thanks." He handed the kid a ten-dollar bill. "You've been a big help."

"Hey, thanks yourself, man," the kid said, and dragged up the hem of his T-shirt to stuff the bill into the pocket of his baggy shorts.

Steve turned back to Willow. "Think you can make it across under your own power, sweetheart?" he said, indicating the street with a tilt of his head. "Or would you like me to carry you?"

Willow smiled and slipped her hand into the crook of his elbow. "I'll walk," she said dryly, and then leaned her head against his shoulder for support. "You lead the way."

9

WILLOW HAD NOTICED the blood soaking through the lower right leg of Steve's jeans by the time they made it up the narrow staircase and into his office. She tried to insist that he sit on the sofa and wait while she went down the hall to the washroom and brought back a wet cloth but he wouldn't hear of it. They ended up going down to the washroom together. It was one of those old-fashioned ones with a pedestal sink, a dispenser of continuous-loop cloth toweling and ugly green tile running halfway up the walls. Using one of the clean towels he kept in the lowest drawer of his filing cabinet as a washcloth, they took turns cleaning each other's wounds.

He dabbed at the shallow abrasions on her elbows first, gently cleaning out the clinging bits of dirt while she gritted her teeth and tried not to whimper.

"It'll be all right, sweetheart," he crooned, keeping up a steady stream of soothing words while he worked over her, as if she were a child who needed to be reassured. "I'm almost finished. Just a little bit more now," he murmured, stopping every minute or so to make sure it wasn't too much for her to bear.

And then it was her turn to minister to him.

"I think you ought to have stitches in this," Willow said, on her knees behind him as she dabbed at the wound on his leg through the jagged tear in his jeans.

"Is it still bleeding?"

"No." She dabbed at it again, gently, being careful not to disturb the crust that was already forming. "But it looks awful. It'll heal all jagged if you don't get it stitched up."

"As long as it's not bleeding, it's fine," he said, twisting around to look down at it. "I wish you'd get the hell up from there." He frowned at her, leaning over to hook a hand under her arm and pull her up. "You'll ruin your dress on that floor. It's probably not as clean as it should be."

She had to smile at that. "My dress is already ruined," she said wryly. "In a contest between silk and asphalt, silk'll lose every time. Guaranteed."

He glanced down, noticing for the first time that her pretty print dress was ripped down one side. Without asking permission, he pushed the fabric out of the way to examine her leg for damage. Her panty hose were shredded across her outer thigh, as if they'd been pulled over a grater. The skin beneath looked red and raw. Before she knew what was happening, he had both hands up under her dress.

"What are you doing?" she squealed in alarm, grabbing at his hands through the slippery silk.

"Getting rid of these panty hose. I need to see how bad your leg is."

"All right," she said, knowing she wasn't going to dissuade him once he'd decided on a course of action. "But I'll do it."

The way he was going about it, she'd end up losing her underpants as well as her panty hose. And if that happened, she suspected their first time would be in a grubby little public washroom up against a tiled wall. While that had a certain rough appeal, she didn't think she was up to it at the moment—and never mind that it wasn't the setting she'd pictured when she thought about making love with Steve for the first time.

"I have to take my shoes off first," she said, lifting her foot to rest it on the edge of the toilet. She nearly lost her balance when she leaned over to unbuckle the T-strap.

Steve reached out to steady her, righting her before she had a chance to do more than totter. "What's the matter?" he demanded, fear for her making his voice harsh. "Do you feel faint?"

"I just got a little dizzy when I bent over like that. I'm all right now."

"It's not all right, damn it. Here—" he took her hands and put them on the edge of the sink "—hold on to this while I get your shoes off." He sank down on one knee, lifting her left foot, and then her right, up on his other knee to unbuckle her shoes and slip them off. "Okay," he said, looking up at her from his position at her feet. "Let's peel those panty hose down."

Willow thought fleetingly of her vow to have him on his knees, but this wasn't exactly what she'd had in mind. "Turn around," she ordered.

"Oh, for cryin' out loud," he burst out. "It's not like I haven't seen a woman take off her panty hose before."

"You haven't seen *this* woman take off her panty hose," she said stubbornly, a touch of asperity in her voice. "And if you don't cooperate now, you may *never* see me take them off," she threatened, not realizing the promise implicit in her words. She made a little circling motion with her index finger. "Turn around."

With a reluctant grin, Steve got to his feet and turned around.

Willow flicked up the sides of her skirt, slipped her fingers under the waistband of her ruined panty hose, and pushed them down to her thighs. Her breath hissed out through her teeth as nylon scrapped over the tender skin of her left thigh. "Not yet," she said when Steve started to turn. "I'll tell you when."

She eased the shredded nylon down past the scraped area and then leaned against the sink, balancing herself with one hand at a time as she lifted each knee in turn to push the hose off over her feet without bending her head. "Okay," she said, as she dropped them in the trash can.

There was no way she could stop him from tending to the wound himself, and she didn't even try. Pulling the edge of her ripped skirt up and back with one hand, she held it out of the way while he dabbed at the affected area with the wet towel.

"It's just a friction burn," he assured her, pressing the cool, damp fabric against her thigh with the flat of his hand to soothe it. "Nowhere near as bad as the scrapes on your elbows. It'll be a little tender for a day or two and you'll probably have a bruise but that's all."

"Good," she murmured, letting the skirt fall back into place as she moved away from him. "I guess we're finished in here, then, aren't we?" She bent over to pick up her shoes as she spoke, forgetting about the dizziness that seemed to strike whenever she lowered her head.

The next thing she knew she was lying on the sofa in Steve's office with his hands gently moving through her hair, her eyes and forehead covered by a wet cloth that was dribbling rivulets of cold water into her ears and down her neck. She lifted her hand to push it away.

"Lie still," Steve ordered, holding her down by putting one hand in the middle of her chest when she tried to sit up.

"You're drowning me," she complained, struggling against his hold. "Let me up."

"All right. Take it easy." He took the wet towel from her head and dropped it on the floor. "Just lie still for another minute," he said, as he continued to move his hands over her head. "Tender?" he asked, when she flinched.

"A little."

"There's no bump but I think we should take you to the hospital to have a doctor look you over, just in case."

"No hospital," Willow insisted. "I'll be fine. Really. I've had much worse falls while riding," she reassured him. "Let me sit up."

He slipped his arm under her neck, carefully cradling her head against his shoulder. "Slowly," he murmured as he lifted her upright. "Okay?" he asked, his gaze on her face, watching for the slightest sign that she might be going to faint again.

"Okay," she agreed, with a tiny, careful nod, testing to see how her head felt.

"Don't you *ever* do that to me again," he ordered fiercely.

Her eyes widened at the vehemence in his tone. "I didn't exactly do it on purpose," she pointed out.

"Well, just don't do it again. You nearly scared the life out of me."

"Sorry," she murmured. "I'll try not to keel over in front of you again."

"See that you don't," he said, completely missing the wry edge to her tone as he stood and headed for his office door. "I'm going to go get your shoes. Don't move an inch until I get back."

Willow did as he ordered only because—she told herself—it was the prudent thing to do. While he was gone, she took the opportunity to tilt her head, carefully, from side to side and back and forth. There was a little light-headedness but as long as she didn't move too fast the dizziness didn't return. She'd probably have a whopper of a headache later but she'd live.

She was just about to stand up and test herself a little further, when Steve came back into the room with her shoes. Wisely, she stayed where she was, docilely allowing him to, once again, kneel at her feet while he buckled the scuffed T-straps on for her.

"Do you think you can stand up?" he asked when he finished.

"I think I can manage," she said dryly.

He helped her to her feet as if she were an invalid, holding on to her until it became apparent that she could, indeed, stand up under her own power. Leaving her alone by the sofa for a moment, he gathered up her jacket and purse, and then came back. "Let's get you to a hospital," he said, wrapping his arm around her shoulders to lead her toward the door.

Willow stopped dead in her tracks. "No hospital. If I go to a hospital, they'll want to keep me overnight for observation. I'm not doing that."

"Damn it, Willow, you *fainted*."

"I didn't faint," she said, indignantly. "I got a little dizzy and *you* overreacted."

"You could have a concussion."

"I don't have a concussion," she assured him. "Trust me. I've had concussions before and I know what they feel like." She sighed with exasperation. It was nice to be coddled and fussed over. Very nice. But enough was enough; she'd told him before that she wasn't some fragile flower. "Look, Steve, I appreciate your concern. I really do. But I'm fine. All I need is a hot shower, a little room service and a good night's sleep."

He considered that for a moment. "All right, fine," he agreed, and started her toward the door again. "I'll take you to my place. You can get everything you need there."

"Your place?" She felt a frisson of . . . something . . . slither down her spine, despite the fact that she was in no condition to deal with it at the moment. "Why your place? What's wrong with my hotel room?"

"You'd be alone in your hotel room. What if you fainted in the shower?" he challenged her. "What if you're wrong and you do have a concussion?" *What if the person who tried to run you down decides to try something else?* "You need someone around to check on you every couple of hours throughout the night. It's either me or the doctors over at the UCLA Med Center," he said, a look of bulldog stubbornness on his handsome face. "Take your pick."

Willow made a split-second executive decision. "Okay, we'll go to your place."

STEVE'S PLACE turned out to be a far cry from what Willow expected. Instead of some dinky efficiency apartment in one of the apartment buildings near his office, he drove her to an isolated house in the Santa Monica foothills, just off Laurel Canyon Boulevard. It wasn't much to look at from the outside: simple, rugged, unprepossessing, with thick adobe walls and a low, red-tiled roof. The landscaping had been left mostly to Mother Nature, sweet-smelling wild grasses, chaparral and native scrub had been deliberately left to mix with the cultivated greenery around the house, the boundaries of the garden areas marked by meandering borders of large rocks.

It reminded Willow a little of where she had grown up. Not the vegetation, exactly—there was more pine and evergreen on Blackberry Meadows' isolated mountain acreage—but the feeling. Rural and a little bit wild. Her town house in Portland was in the heart of the city, convenient to everything, and she liked it well enough. But, sometimes, she missed the peaceful solitude of a setting like this.

As she stepped out of the car, Willow heard a coyote howl, off in the distance. She glanced toward the sound, and then up at Steve. "But you're so close to the city," she said, amazed.

"I know. Isn't it great?" He grinned, showing his dimple. "I get deer out here, too. And raccoons and owls. And there's a pair of red-tailed hawks that hunt for their breakfast from that stand of trees every morning." He pointed to a small copse of eucalyptus, their silvery green leaves rustling in a light evening breeze. "Come on inside," he said, guiding her up the path to the front door, "and let's get you settled in."

The inside of the house was an even bigger surprise than the outside had been. It seemed, at first, to be one big open space, with a high, beamed ceiling, bare wood floor, acres of windows that let in the pink glow of the setting sun and a huge fireplace at one end. But a closer look revealed that it was divided into cooking, dining and living spaces by two tiled counters and the clever arrangement of furniture and area rugs.

"Did you do all this yourself?" she asked, wondering if there might have been a wife or live-in love somewhere in his past.

"I worked with the architect on the plans and picked out the furniture," he said, taking her purse and jacket from her to set them down on one of the counters. "But my sister Laurie helped me with the dishes and towels and all that decorating stuff." He waved a hand around, silently indicating the urns full of fragrant eucalyptus, the woven baskets that held magazines and kindling, the knitted throw over the back of a sofa, the tall wrought-iron candlesticks on the wooden dining table.

"It's really lovely. I'm impressed."

"It's comfortable," he allowed, watching her move around the main room of his house, wondering how she would feel about sharing it with him for the rest of their natural lives. He wanted to ask her right now. Wanted to tell her she could change anything she wanted. Wanted to tell her they'd sell it and start over if she didn't like it. Wanted . . . But it was too soon. Way too soon. They had other matters to settle first. "Do you want to eat first, or take that shower?" he asked instead.

"Shower," she said. "I had a cup of coffee and a piece of baklava at the Greek deli before—"

"Before some idiot driver almost ran you down," he finished for her, not wanting her to spend too much time dwelling on what had happened. It would be better for her, easier, if she didn't have to come face-to-face with the knowledge that what had happened probably hadn't been an accident.

"Let me show you where the shower is." He reached out to take her elbow, then remembered in time and took her by the hand, instead, linking his fingers with hers as he led her across the great room to one of the arched doorways opening off of it.

They walked down a short hall, then turned and entered a large airy bedroom done in desert shades of beige and tan and dusty blue. There was a king-size bed under a skylight, wide-paned glass doors leading to a lattice-covered deck, and an adobe fireplace in the corner. "You'll have to use my bathroom," he said, motioning toward the half-open door across the room. "It's the only one that's fully stocked."

"I don't want to put you out of your own bathroom," she said. "Just give me a bar of soap and a towel and point me to a guest bath. I'll be fine."

"You're not putting me out. All I have to do is dig up a clean pair of jeans and I'm set." Unable to resist, he lifted their clasped hands, turning them to place a kiss on the back of her wrist before he untangled his fingers from hers.

Willow felt a sudden attack of dizziness come over her that had nothing to do with the hit she'd taken to her head. She leaned a shoulder against the doorjamb, watching as he moved to the tall bleached-wood dresser against the wall.

"I can offer you sweatpants and a T-shirt to put on after your shower," he said, pulling the items in question from a drawer as he spoke. "Or there's a robe hanging on the back of the door in the bathroom, if you'd rather wear that."

"Sweatpants and a T-shirt will be fine."

"Help yourself to anything you need in the bathroom. The new toothbrushes are on the top shelf of the linen closet. And there's aspirin in the medicine cabinet." He put the clothes in her hands. "I'd suggest you take a couple of them. If you're not aching yet, you will be. Almost getting run over will do that to you."

Oh, I'm aching, all right, Willow thought as she stood there, staring up at him. But it didn't have anything to do with nearly getting run over.

"Are you going to be all right in there by yourself?"

"What?" She blinked. "Oh, yes. Fine. I'll be fine."

"I'll be right outside the door." He ran the backs of his fingers down her cheek, ostensibly brushing a stray hair out of her face. "Holler if you need me."

HOLLER if you need me.

And just what would he do if she did? Willow wondered. Come striding into the shower like a knight in shining armor and . . . wash her back? She faltered a bit at the thought, nearly dropping the soap, wondering if she dared test him that far, wondering if . . . No, she was thinking crazy again; what *was* it about that man that made her want to listen to her hormones instead of her head? It was too soon for that kind of intimacy.

The same sound arguments that applied last night after his refusal had forced her to come to her senses still applied. For all the instant chemistry and surprising affinity of mind they seemed to share, she barely knew him. Even though she accepted the inevitability of an intimate relationship with him—because he was right, it *was* going to happen—two days' acquaintance wasn't long enough for a smart woman like her to risk sharing the secrets of her body with a man. Not to mention those of her heart and soul . . .

STEVE STOOD OUTSIDE the bathroom door with his fists clenched, listening to the sounds of the woman he wanted with every fiber of his being taking a shower in his bathroom. She was standing in *his* shower. Using *his* soap. Sliding *his* washcloth over the sleek, naked curves of her body.

He closed his eyes, imagining how it would be if he joined her in the shower, remembering the feel and taste of her breasts. The way her hips had moved in mindless need against his. The shuddering breaths and little gasping noises she made. The way her arms had clasped him and held him close, wanting him as much as he wanted her.

He lifted his hand, reaching for the doorknob, his whole body urging him to go in and take what he knew she would willingly give him. He would pull back the shower curtain and she would turn, not really startled to see him, *expecting* to see him, and she would lift her arms toward him, her eyes burning with passion and need and fierce feminine welcome.

He was so attuned to her responses, so sure of how she would react, that it was hard to remember he'd only known her for two days. Hard to remember that she was a client who'd come to him looking for help. Hard to remember she'd been battered and bruised and probably wasn't up to the sort of fast and furious sex he was aching to give her. It was hard, period.

He dropped his hand, waiting silently, tensely, for the shower to stop. When it did, he lifted his fist and rapped sharply on the door. "Everything okay in there?" he asked, his voice low and gravelly. "You still on your feet?"

"Don't come in!" she called, an edge of panicked excitement in her voice, and he knew she had been imagining things, too. "I'll be out as soon as I get dressed and dry my hair."

"Take your time," he said, his mind automatically forming a picture of her standing there, dripping water on his blue bathroom rug, one of his striped towels clutched to her breasts as she stared at the door. "I'll be in the kitchen, throwing some sandwiches together. They'll be ready whenever you are."

THEY SAT ACROSS the dining table from each other, eating vegetable soup and grilled-cheese sandwiches. She had blow-dried her hair with his dryer, used the antiseptic spray she found in his medicine cabinet on her elbows and thigh, just to be on the safe side, and taken two aspirin as he had suggested to forestall the headache that hadn't yet developed. She felt clean and cozy, and ridiculously coddled, dressed in a pair of his sweatpants and a pale blue T-shirt that hung halfway down her thighs.

"Okay," she said, waiting until he had taken a healthy bite of his cheese sandwich before she spoke. "Spill it."

Steve chewed and swallowed. "Spill what?" he asked, reaching for his iced tea to help wash the sandwich down.

"This house," she said, gesturing at the room with her soupspoon. "The office on Hollywood Boulevard. You've got to admit they don't go together."

"Why not?" he asked blandly.

"Don't give me that look," she said. "You know why not. Your office belongs to a semisuccessful P.I. who's just about managing to make ends meet. Your books, by the way, tell the same story. This place was built by someone with money." And taste, but she didn't tell him that. "Lots and lots of money. Either you've got a really successful—and, therefore, probably illegal— sideline going, or some rich Los Angeles socialite has you on retainer for something other than your skill as an investigator," she said with a sly grin, deliberately choosing the two possibilities that would be most likely to get a rise out of him.

He didn't take the bait. "Maybe I'm independently wealthy."

"Are you?"

"Would it make a difference if I was?"

"To what?" she said, puzzled by the question.

"To you."

"To me?" It took her a minute to understand what he was getting at. And then her eyes narrowed, snapping fire. She started to rise up out of her chair.

"Gotcha," he said, and grinned at her.

She gave him a mutinous glare and sat back down. "That wasn't funny," she said.

"Sure it was. You're just mad because I didn't react when you tried to insult me."

She ducked her head, hiding a grin as she bit into her sandwich. He was right, damn him! How had he learned to read her so well in just two short days? She swallowed her bite of sandwich. "So, are you really independently wealthy?"

"Yes, I really am."

She tilted her head, her eyes speculative as she stared at him across the table. "I don't see how," she said. "You're an abysmal businessman who hasn't got the slightest idea of how to keep a proper set of books."

"I have a trust fund," he said, not the least bit offended by what she obviously thought he would consider a major insult. "My sister Laurie manages it for me. She's an investment banker."

"You're kidding."

"No, really, she is."

Willow gave him a wry look, letting him know that she knew that *he* knew that hadn't been what she meant. "Where did a semisuccessful P.I. get a trust fund?"

"My mother's maiden name was Fallon. Her family used to own quite a lot of what was once arid farmland in the San Fernando Valley, way back before the Aqueduct was built in the early 1900s. Down through the years they've managed to hang on to most of it. Only now it's tract homes and shopping centers and light industry."

Willow was silent for a moment, considering that. She'd never heard of the Fallons but she knew what it meant to have owned land in the Valley before it became the home of some one-third of Los Angeles's entire population. And to still own it now.

"And your father's family? Did they give you a tidy little trust fund, too?"

"Mom married down," he said with a grin. "My dad is William S. Hart, the attorney."

She might not have heard of the Fallons but she knew who William S. Hart was. The famous civil rights lawyer had retired a few years ago, if she remembered rightly, after having made a name for himself as a fireeater who often took on seemingly lost-cause cases that other lawyers saw no profit in.

"So that explains the house," Willow said, "but how do you explain the business you're in?"

"Does it need explaining?"

"Sure. I mean, with a background like that, why aren't you some high-priced lawyer with a Harvard degree and an office in Beverly Hills?"

"I was. The Harvard degree part," he said, amused by her thunderstruck expression. "Not the Beverly Hills part."

"What happened?"

"Lawyers have to play by the rules." He shrugged. "I like to do things my own way."

Willow didn't doubt that for a minute but there was more to it than that. A lot more. "And?" she prodded.

"And what?"

"That still doesn't explain why you do what you do, or why your office is located in a low-rent building on Hollywood Boulevard."

"I do what I do because I'm good at it, and I like it," he said, dismissively. "And my office is where it is because that's where most of my clients are."

Willow stared at him across the table, a considering look in her golden brown eyes. He could see the wheels turning as she tried to fit the pieces together. And then she pursed her lips and nodded, as if to herself, and her eyes widened. The look she gave him had him squirming in embarrassment.

"You're a big ol' fake," she said softly, as the truth dawned on her. "You're not a tough guy at all. You're a marshmallow underneath all those muscles. An idealist. A crusader."

"Knock it off," he grumbled, and buried his nose in his iced tea to keep her from seeing that his cheeks were turning pink.

But Willow had sharp eyes, and an even sharper tongue. She couldn't resist. He was so cute when he blushed. "You're a savior of lost children," she said. "A defender of women," she added, thinking of herself. "A righter of wrongs. A superhero fighting for truth, justice and the American way on the mean streets of L.A."

Steve put down the glass and met her gaze across the table, trying to stare her into backing off. She met his gaze unflinchingly, her eyes soft and glowing, bright with admiration . . . and something else. They stared at each other for an aeons-long second, both of them suddenly breathing too fast, their hearts pounding too hard, their blood heated and screaming through their veins, both of them hovering on the brink of . . . something.

"A modern warrior knight with his own code of honor," Willow said, the teasing note all but gone from her voice. "A grown-up Boy Scout."

"Willow, damn it, I'm warning you . . ." he growled but it was an empty threat and they both knew it. He would no more hurt her than he would hurt a child. "That's enough."

"Whad'a'ya gonna do, tough guy?" Willow challenged.

With a groan, he reached out, grabbing her by her shoulders, and dragged her across the table into his arms.

10

HE TOOK HER LIPS in a powerful, punishing kiss, pushed beyond gentleness by two days of more frustration than man should ever have to endure. Willow answered him with a power of her own, wrapping her arms around his waist as his went around her back, rising up on her knees on the table to get even closer, opening her mouth to his ravaging tongue as her head fell back under the passionate onslaught of his lips.

The kiss went on forever, their lips sliding wetly against each other's, their heads turning and tilting to find the best, the most satisfying angle. Teeth nibbling and nipping. Tongues tasting and dueling. Hot, intemperate, desperate, endless kisses with his hands sliding through her hair to hold her head, and her fingers gripping the back of his soft cotton T-shirt to keep him from moving even one tiny centimeter away.

Willow could feel something soft, squishing beneath her knee, and realized, vaguely, that it was the remains of his cheese sandwich. Steve could feel the warmth of spilled soup, soaking into the leg of his jeans as it trickled off the edge of the table. Neither of them cared for such mundane considerations.

All that mattered was satisfying the need that had started building between them from almost the minute they first looked at each other. The need that had been growing voraciously, second by second, minute by minute, hour by hour, until it seemed to be the only thing in the world that mattered. After two days of mental foreplay and their own fevered imaginings, there was, finally, only one way to relieve the terrible tension inside them. They had to get closer . . . ever closer . . . closer still. Without conscious thought they began to undress each other.

She released her death grip on his T-shirt and slid her hands around to his front, reaching down to fumble with his belt buckle and the metal buttons on the strained fly of his jeans.

He moved his hands down her back, sliding them down the curve of her spine, slipping under the waistband of the loose navy sweatpants she wore. Cupping his hands, gliding them over the firm, fleshy curves of her bare bottom, he skimmed the backs of her thighs as he pushed the soft fleece fabric down. With his mouth still fastened to hers, he curled his fingers around the backs of her knees, lifting slightly, pulling them forward so that she ended up sitting on the edge of the table with her bare legs dangling over the side, sweatpants and smashed cheese sandwich on the floor between his feet.

She freed the last button on his jeans and slipped her hands, palms flat against his narrow hips, inside both jeans and briefs to push them down.

He gasped into her mouth, a hoarse ragged sound, his big, hard body shuddering with intemperate, overwhelming, mindless need as his erection sprang free.

She wrapped her fingers around him in blatant demand, leaning backward to pull him down on top of her.

He yanked her forward, his hands hard on her thighs.

She flinched.

He stopped.

Willow tore her mouth from his. "I swear to God," she murmured raggedly, her voice shaking with need, "if you stop now, I'll kill you with my bare hands."

He leaned forward, curling an arm around her back for support, and swept the rest of the debris off the table with one arm, sending glasses, crockery and cutlery crashing to the floor. Then, in one smooth motion, he slid her back into position and levered himself up onto the table between her legs.

"To stop me now, you'd *have* to kill me," he replied, and thrust himself into her.

Willow made a wild exultant sound, deep in her throat, and lifted her legs, wrapping them around his waist as he began to move in her. She clutched at his shoulders with both hands, her fingers curled tightly in the soft fabric of his T-shirt, holding on for dear life as he tried to get closer to her than was humanly possible with each driving thrust.

She could hear the hoarse sloughing of his breath; feel the wild pounding of his heart; see the trembling in his powerful arms as he struggled to give her what she needed before he took what he so desperately desired for himself.

It was reckless and untamed.

It was fast and furious and frantic.

It was primitive, unrestrained sex at its most basic.

It was *glorious*.

Willow arched her back in voluptuous, victorious surrender, pressing her head against the table, and let completion take her. A high, keening sound of feminine triumph burst from her throat at the peak, releasing Steve to find his own fierce satisfaction. He took it with a guttural cry of masculine conquest and triumph that matched hers, sinking down to capture her mouth with his for a deep, carnal kiss as the last shudders racked his body.

It was several long, lazy delicious minutes later before they even began to surface. Willow came back to herself first, becoming aware of the puddle of cold tea soaking through her T-shirt between her shoulder blades, and the hardness of the table beneath her, and the various aches and pains that came from indulging in unbridled passion on a surface not intended for the purpose. She smiled, wanton and unrepentant, already relishing the memory of those mad, sweet moments.

She might have a few more bruises tomorrow to add to the scrapes she'd received earlier but it had been worth it. More than worth it. She turned her head, pressing a soft kiss to the warm skin below his ear, and whispered his name.

Steve sighed and lifted his head from the fragrant curve of her neck to look down at her. "Are you all right?"

"Mmm-hmm," she murmured and smiled up at him, her eyes half-closed and slumberous.

She really has the most remarkably expressive eyes, he thought as he stared down at her. They showed every passing thought and emotion. They were by turns vulnerable and trusting; wide with astonishment; snapping with anger or indignation; brimming with laughter and a sly teasing wit that challenged both his intellect and his manhood; soft and hot and aching with need; glowing with sweet satisfaction as they were now.

He wondered how they would look when she tumbled into love, and how long he would have to wait before he would see that look in her eyes. He would wait however long it took, of course. He'd committed himself to her, here on his dining table. No, that wasn't quite true; he'd committed himself this afternoon when he'd caught sight of her coming out of Christo's Deli and felt his heart stop beating in his chest for one breathless moment. Otherwise, no matter how frustrated he was, or how much she'd teased him, this wouldn't have happened while she was still his client—at least, that's what he tried to tell himself.

It had been more than just the buildup of frustration and desire, more than their brush with death. For him, their wild lovemaking had been the physical confirmation of his feelings. He hadn't meant to do it so soon—or in such a graceless way!—but what was done was done and he couldn't find it in himself to be sorry. He wasn't going to beat himself up over it, either. He'd staked his claim. She was his now, to care for and to cherish and to love. Sooner or later, she would realize it for herself. He could wait until she did. If he didn't have to wait too long.

"I hate to break up the party," she said teasingly. "But this table wasn't made for lying on and all this muscle—" she stroked his wide shoulders caressingly, with the flat of both hands "—weighs a ton."

He grinned and lifted himself away from her, reaching down between them as he did so. His grin faded and he swore softly, viciously.

Startled, Willow lifted her head, following his gaze to where their bodies had just been so intimately joined. It took her a minute to realize what the problem was, and then, when she did, she had to bite her lip to keep from laughing.

It wasn't anything to laugh about, really. The whole matter could have deadly serious consequences, but she couldn't help it. The soft giggles escaped against her will.

The careful, conscientious, well-prepared Mr. Hart had forgotten to use protection.

"WE SHOULD TALK about what happened on the table," Steve said, as they lay together in his bed with the moonlight shining down on them through the wide glass doors and the skylight above the bed. They were fresh from another bout of loving, scarcely less frantic and frenzied than first time except that he'd slowed down enough to remember to use the contents of one of the little foil packets stored in the drawer of his bedside table. "You could end up pregnant."

"That's not very likely," Willow assured him. "It's the wrong time of the month."

"But it could happen," he insisted, and laid his hand over her stomach. It covered her entire lower abdomen, from her navel to the dark silky hair below. He imagined placing it in that exact spot, some unspecified number of years or months from now, when her belly was round and ripe with his child. "It could be happening right now," he said, almost wistfully.

Willow shrugged against the pillow, wondering why the thought of being pregnant with his baby wasn't as distressing as it should have been. "Let's not worry about it until there's actually something to worry about," she suggested, trying to keep it light, for both their sakes. "There's no sense borrowing trouble." She touched the back of his hand with the tip of her index finger, tracing a meandering line over the tendons that stood out in bas-relief under his skin. "There are other things we should both be concerned with."

"I'm HIV negative," he said promptly. "I get tested every year, more often if I think I might have had some questionable contact."

"Does that happen often?" Willow asked, startled by the admission of such a free and easy sex life. "Having questionable contacts?"

"In my line of work, you can't be too careful. Sometimes a junkie will bleed on you, or you'll have to give first aid to some kid who's been turning tricks to keep body and soul together."

"Oh," she said, a bit embarrassed at having jumped to the wrong conclusion. "I saw the boxes of condoms in your office and I thought . . ."

"Why, Willow Ryan," he teased, rising up on his elbow to look down at her, "were you snooping in my desk drawers?"

"I was looking for a pencil sharpener," she said primly, hoping he couldn't see her incriminating blush in the shadowed moonlight.

"Uh-huh," he snorted. "You were snooping."

"Don't you want to hear my sexual history?" she asked, in an effort to change the subject.

"Is there something about it I should know?"

"Not really. My first lover was a virgin," she said, wishing he would lie back down so she could give her report a little more . . . anonymously. It was disconcerting to be discussing past lovers with him staring at her face. "My second lover was a boy I met at college. We used condoms."

"And?"

"And that's it," she snapped, unaccountably aggrieved. "My sex life hasn't been as vast and varied as yours obviously has."

He couldn't help but smile. Only two lovers. She wasn't a woman who gave herself lightly or casually. Which made the fact that she'd given herself to him, and after only two days, all the more special. She was half-way in love and didn't even know it.

"I don't see what's so amusing about one of us being an indiscriminate sex fiend," she pouted, reaching up to push him away.

He grabbed her hand, holding it against his bare chest. "While I'll admit I've had a few more than two previous lovers," he said, "there hasn't been some faceless horde parading through my bedroom, either."

"Hah!" she said succinctly and tried to pull her hand away.

He tightened his fingers on hers, refusing to let her go. "I give away most of the condoms I keep in my office."

She stopped trying to pull her hand out of his. "Give them away? To who?" she asked suspiciously.

"To street kids, mostly. Runaways. A lot of them turn tricks to survive. They need all the protection they can get."

"Oh," she said in a small voice.

"Now, the ones I keep in the drawer by the bed, though . . ." he said, waiting until she looked at him. "Those I use myself, and I don't like to let them lie around too long or else they start to deteriorate." He rolled over onto his back, still holding her hand against his chest, and reached out with his other hand, dipping it into the open drawer. "I'd say there are, oh, about a half dozen left." He glanced over at her, his eyes teasing, his dimple flashing in the moonlight. "We've got a busy night ahead of us, sweetheart."

HE TOOK IT SLOWLY, agonizingly slowly, the third time they came together, exploring every inch of her body, learning what merely pleased her and what drove her mad with frenzied, unreasoning desire. His intention was to possess her, totally; to create a bond with his body; to brand her so that every time she thought of making love, she thought of him. He went about it with diabolical thoroughness and consummate skill.

He was lavish with his hands, touching her everywhere, gently stroking her face and the insides of her thighs, cupping her breasts with exquisite care, kneading the curve of her waist and her strong, slender calves and the firm, fleshy swell of her hips, preparing her body for the deeper pleasures to come.

He was exacting and precise with his fingers, using them to gently pinch and pluck at her nipples until they were hard and aching, delicately circling the little nub of flesh between her legs until she was taut and panting, penetrating her deeply, over and over, until she was slick and swollen and twisting mindlessly on the sheets.

He was profligate with his kisses, sprinkling them from her forehead to her toes, lavishing special attention on the sides of her neck, and her aching nipples, and the backs of her knees . . . and the petaled, tumescent flesh between her thighs.

She lost count of the number of times he brought her to climax before she could stand no more and finally demanded equal time by pushing his hands away and rising to her knees beside him.

He lay back, as generous with his body as he had been demanding of hers, making himself vulnerable to her more inexperienced explorations, showing her the motions and caresses that gave him pleasure, then leaving her to experiment and expand them on her own. She was soon drunk on her power over his strong, hard-muscled body. *This* made him quiver. And *this* made him moan. And *this* made him shake with uncontrollable need.

And, then, finally, he, too, had had all he could stand. He rolled onto his side, reaching once again into the drawer of the bedside table. He put the foil packet in her hands this time, letting her open it and unroll it onto his turgid length with eager, shaking fingers. And when it was done, he pulled her astride him, holding himself for her while she lowered her sweetness onto him, enveloping his penis in the exquisite tightness of her feminine sheath.

Her first movements were awkward and uncertain but he put his hands on her hips, showing her the motion. She caught the rhythm and rode him hard, her head thrown back, her breasts thrust out, taking everything he had to give and demanding more. Their climax was explosive and nearly simultaneous, each coming so close upon the other that there was no telling who came first and who followed. He dug his fingers into her hips, holding her tight against his loins, his back rigid and bowed as the last of his body's energy pumped into her. She curled her fingers into the heavy muscles of his chest, leaving scratches in her wake, as her whole body tightened in delicious, agonizing, exquisite ecstasy.

When it was over, she collapsed on his chest in utter exhaustion and he gathered her close, cradling her to him as he rolled over onto his side. She murmured his name, softly, lifting her arm to drape it around his neck and pull herself even closer. Steve smiled and closed his eyes, falling into a deep, contented sleep.

"DO YOU THINK my mother's accident and the hit-and-run yesterday have anything to do with each other?" Willow asked, looking at Steve over the froth of bubbles that separated them. They were sitting in the hot tub tucked in the corner of the deck in his backyard, with tall glasses of fresh-squeezed orange juice close at hand, soaking away the excesses of a passionate night in bed and a long, lazy Sunday morning spent making love all over the house.

Steve looked over at her, then shook his head, wondering why he was even surprised. "Not much gets by you, does it?"

"A speeding car bearing down on you is kind of hard to miss."

His quick grin acknowledged her point, and then he sobered. "How much do you know about what happened to your mother?"

"Just what I told you the other day. She was hit by a car while crossing Hollywood Boulevard. Sharon got a letter from the police department or maybe it was someone from the . . . the morgue where they took her body."

Steve moved over, so that they were sitting side by side instead of across from each other, and slid his arm around her shoulders.

"I guess it took them that long to locate her next of kin," she went on, comforted by his touch, "because we were out of state."

"This letter you got—did it give you any details? Say anything about the accident? Was she jaywalking? Was it a drunk driver? Someone running a red light? A hit-and-run?"

"I don't know." She looked at him, her eyes wide and vulnerable, sure he would know. "*Was* it a hit-and-run?"

"We'll know tomorrow," he promised her. "I called my contact at the LAPD last night while you were in the shower. He's going to look into it for me."

"If it was, then somebody killed her, didn't they?" She said it matter-of-factly, calmly, as if she were talking about a stranger. "And somebody tried to kill me."

"*If*," he emphasized. "But, yes, if all that's true, then it's beginning to look that way."

Willow was silent a moment, coming to terms with that. "Ethan Roberts?"

"We don't know that for sure."

"No, not for sure," she agreed. "But you think it was him." It wasn't a question, but a statement of fact.

"*If* your mother's accident turns out to be a hit-and-run, then, yes, on the basis of what I found out yesterday, I think it very well might be him. Or someone hired by him."

"Tell me," she demanded. "Everything."

"It isn't a pretty story."

"Tell me."

So Steve sighed, and told her.

"Roberts first surfaced in Hollywood in the late sixties. He did a couple of commercials, snagged a few spots as a bit player in a couple of the weekly series on TV at the time. He got his big break in 1970, playing a doctor on 'As Time Goes By.' That's where he met your mother. He told the truth about that as far as it went. The studio did arrange the dates, at least the first one, but it was at Roberts' insistence. According to one of the grips I talked to who still works on the show, it was the only way he could get her to go out with him. That may be sour grapes," Steve cautioned her. "The guy admitted he didn't like Roberts much, said he was on a star trip in a big way and treated the crew as if they were some kind of subhuman species who'd been put on earth for his convenience."

"The way he treats his maid," Willow said.

Steve nodded. "This grip, though, he liked your mother. Said she was a real sweetheart, always friendly toward the crew, always prepared and professional. He said he was real sorry when she left the show. Everyone thought she had a lot of potential."

Willow reached up and squeezed the hand that curved over her bare shoulder, silently thanking him.

"Anyway, Roberts quit the show in 1972 after hitting it big as the the upright, clean-cut hero in a couple of low-budget Westerns that were a surprise hit at the box office."

"I remember those," Willow said. "They play on TV every now and then. On the Family Channel."

"He married his costar from one of those movies in 1977, a young actress named Heather Blaine. She had their first son, Peter, seven months later. Edward was born in 1979 and they were divorced before he was a year old. Roberts continued to make movies, becoming more and more successful without ever actually achieving the status of a really big star, like, say, Nicholson or Eastwood. It was enough to make him very, very wealthy, though. Meanwhile—" Steve's jaw clenched with anger "—his ex-wife and kids were living in a two-bedroom apartment in West Hollywood and struggling to make ends meet."

Willow's hand tightened on Steve's, reflecting his feelings, telegraphing her own. Without lifting his palm from her shoulder, he spread his fingers, linking them through hers.

"By '82, his star looked like it was beginning to fade," he went on. "He hadn't made a movie in a while and was doing cameos and guest appearances on television. Then, in 1984, he met Joanna Hudson, the daughter of local political bigwig, Blake Hudson, at some local charity thing. The three of them apparently hit it off. With Hudson's backing, Roberts ran for his first political office in '85 and won a seat on the L.A. city board by a wide margin. He and Joanna married the following year and, by all accounts, his father-in-law started grooming him for bigger and better things. In 1986, before he announced his campaign for a seat in the California House of Representatives, Roberts began a custody battle for his two sons. It was very nasty. His ex-wife didn't have a chance. Roberts' high-priced team of lawyers produced witnesses who claimed she was a junkie who had traded sex for drugs, sometimes in front of the boys. It was believable because Heather had a history of drug problems, back before her first son was born. And she admitted to accepting gifts of money from men to help make ends meet, but she swore that she'd never brought them into the apartment. She had friends who testified to that in court, who said she was a good mother, doing the best she could for her kids, with no help from their father. The local press ate it up, of course, making Roberts out to be this avenging angel swooping down to save his kids from their drug-addicted slut of a mother. When the judge gave full custody of the boys to Roberts, Heather apparently went berserk, screaming about how she wasn't going to let him get away with it, how she was going to expose him for what he really was and get her boys back if it was the last thing she did. It took two bailiffs to drag her out of the courtroom. The day after the boys were taken away, Heather was found dead of an overdose in the bathroom of her apartment."

"Suicide?" Willow whispered hopefully.

"Maybe." Steve reached for his glass of orange juice with his free hand and took a long drink, trying to wash the bitter taste out of his mouth. "Or maybe she was just an impediment to be gotten rid of."

"Like my mother," Willow said softly, horror making her voice barely audible. She shuddered. "Like me."

Steve put his glass of orange juice down on the edge of the tub and reached for her, dragging her onto his lap and into his arms. "We don't know that for sure," he said, lifting his hand to tuck a strand of wet hair behind her ear. "Your mother's death may have been an accident."

"And yesterday, was that an accident, too? Was that little boy wrong in thinking the driver tried to run me down?"

"No." Steve shook his head, wishing he could reassure her, knowing he couldn't. The minute he'd seen the car bearing down on her, he'd somehow *felt* the intent of the driver. The kid's words just confirmed what he already knew. "Whoever was driving that car was trying to kill you," he said.

Willow closed her eyes for a moment, fighting tears and panic. "What if he's my father?"

"He might not be. Odds are, he isn't," Steve said, trying to wipe that stark, horrified look out of her eyes. "We could find something in that box of Jack Shannon's that proves he isn't, and Eric Shannon is. Or maybe it'll turn out to be Blackstone. Or maybe it's someone else entirely. Someone we don't even know about. It doesn't have to be Ethan Roberts."

"But you think it is. And you think he tried to kill me because I could be an impediment to his career, too."

Steve was silent, unable to give her the answer she wanted, unable to lie.

Willow's control broke. She dropped her head to his shoulder and started to cry.

11

STEVE WRAPPED HIS ARMS tightly around her and held her close, stroking her hair, cradling her like a beloved and grieving child. He didn't offer mindless platitudes or soothing words; there were none to offer. He simply held her while she cried, slowly rocking her back and forth while the warm, bubbly water swirled around them. She stopped after a few minutes, sniffling into his neck as she struggled to control herself. And then, even that soft noise stopped and she fell silent, her body limp against him. He thought she'd fallen asleep, like a child exhausted by the passion of her tears, but she sighed raggedly, drawing in the breath to speak.

"When I was a little girl," she said, the words so softly spoken that he had to strain to hear them, "I used to make up all these wild, improbable stories to explain to myself why I didn't have a father. The details changed over the years but the one constant was that he hadn't abandoned my mother and me by choice, that something beyond his control had taken him away, and that he really had loved us. I knew I wasn't going to find that tragic fairy-tale hero when I finally came looking for him," she admitted. "And maybe that's why I waited so long to begin the search. But I thought..." Her shoulders lifted in a little shrug. "I don't know, I guess

I thought I'd find some regular kind of guy, somebody who'd once been in love with a beautiful young woman but it didn't work out. Someone who might even be glad to know he had a daughter." She lifted her head to look at him, the expression in her eyes piteous and vulnerable, asking for reassurance. "I didn't think I'd find a monster."

Steve cupped her face in his hands. "It doesn't make any difference, one way or the other, whether Ethan Roberts is your father or not," he said softly, brushing at the remnants of her tears with his thumbs. "He didn't have anything to do with who you are and what you've become. That pleasure belongs to your aunt Sharon and uncle Dan, and the rest of the people who raised you. You are who you are because of them. Not because of some guy who may or may not have donated a sperm cell."

"I know that," Willow said. "I really do. Finding out who my father is—even if it is Ethan Roberts—isn't going to change my life, or who I am. I didn't expect it to. It's just . . ."

She shrugged and sat up in his lap, smiling crookedly, embarrassed by her tears, dismayed by the loss of her childhood dreams, frightened by the ugly possibilities looming in the future, determined to face what came with her head up and her back straight.

"The whole thing's kind of knocked me for a loop," she said, trying for a semblance of her usual light-hearted flippancy.

Steve was unbearably moved by her courage. Emotion swelled in his chest, threatening to choke him. "I love you," he said, wanting to give her something to replace what she'd lost.

Willow's eyes widened until they threatened to fill up her whole face. Of all the things he could have said to her, that was the last thing she had expected. Coming on top of all the other shocks she'd had in the last few days, it was almost too much to take in. "I don't know what to say," she murmured, finally, unable to give him anything but the truth.

"You don't have to say anything," he said. "I just wanted you to know."

He stood then, and set her on her feet in the tub. "We'd better go in and get dressed," he said, as casually as if he hadn't just made one of the most incredible declarations she'd ever heard. "Zeke Blackstone is expecting us at four and we have to stop by your hotel first and get you checked out."

ZEKE BLACKSTONE was something of a Hollywood legend. He'd come to California from off Off Broadway in New York at the age of twenty-two, lured by promises of fame and fortune on the silver screen. His sizzling performance in his very first movie had fulfilled that dream, catapulting him into the movie star stratosphere, and he'd resided there ever since. Now, at age forty-seven, he was in his prime, both professionally and personally, directing and producing as well as playing romantic leads opposite women less than half his age.

He lived with his wife, television star Ariel Cameron, in a house just off of the Pacific Coast Highway in a private and very exclusive beach community formally known as the Malibu Beach Colony but called, simply, The Colony, by those in the know.

Expecting breathtaking views of the ocean, fabulous shopping arcades where the rich and famous bought their Armani, Evian and imported goat cheese, and million-dollar estates, Willow was disappointed in the actuality. The only views of the Pacific were those that could be glimpsed between buildings and foliage, the shopping was mostly ordinary strip malls, and the estates—if they were there at all—were hidden behind security gates and tall, weathered fences.

"Are you sure this is it?" Willow asked as they turned down a narrow road that supposedly led to Zeke Blackstone's beachfront home.

Steve gave her a knowing glance. "Trust me," he said as he nosed the Mustang into a wide blacktop driveway in front of what looked like a simple suburban garage. Tall overgrown hedges that appeared not to have seen a pair of gardener's shears in months rose up on both sides of the driveway, blocking the view of the beach and partially obscuring the walkway to the narrow set of steep wooden steps leading up to the front door—which was weathered and blue and badly in need of paint.

Ariel Cameron answered the door herself, looking as cool and elegant as she did on television. Her hair was as pale and golden as it appeared on TV, worn sleek and smooth with the ends turning under just before they reached her shoulders. Her eyes were big and blue, her slender figure was stunning.

She was barefoot, wearing a pair of slim white jeans, a white cotton tunic sweater and tiny pearl studs in her ears. A diamond the size of a small ice cube glittered on her left hand.

"Zeke's out on the deck," she said when they had introduced themselves. "Please, come in."

They followed her through a house that lived up to every expectation Willow had ever had about the way movie stars lived. The foyer was larger than her Portland living room, triangular in shape, with an abstract metal chandelier hanging from the apex of the canted cathedral ceiling and a three-panel Andy Warhol silk screen of Ariel Cameron's fabulous face on the wall.

The living room was two steps down, the textured pale gray slate floor of the foyer giving way to smooth bleached wood. The furniture was overstuffed and oversize, big cushy sofas and chairs upholstered in white, cream and ivory with dozens of fat pillows in delicate shades of the palest pinks, blues, yellows and greens. Large Turkish carpets echoed the pastel color scheme while defining the separate conversational areas. The coffee tables were large, square and low, made of pale wood and squares of beveled glass. There was a huge fieldstone fireplace at one end of the room and a grand piano at the other, which still left enough room for a hundred people to have a party. The entire wall on the west side of the house, facing the beach, was glass.

Through it, they could see a man leaning against the railing of the wooden deck, talking on a cellular phone. Ariel rapped on the glass to get his attention. He looked up and smiled, holding up one finger to indicate he'd be a moment longer, and went back to his conversation.

"Sit down, please," Ariel said, indicating the nearest conversational grouping. "I'm going to run out to the kitchen and get us all something to drink. Is wine all right or would you prefer something else?"

"Wine's fine," Steve said.

"Can I help you with anything?" Willow asked automatically, because that's the way she'd been raised.

Ariel smiled. "No, thank you. I can manage." She glanced toward the glass door as it slid open. "Here comes Zeke now."

Zeke Blackstone was as gorgeous as his wife: tall and broad shouldered, nearly as dark as she was blond, with coffee brown eyes and a thick shaggy mane of hair that was just barely touched with gray at the temples. His jeans were faded and blue, his shirt was rumpled white linen and he wore battered Sperry Top-Sider deck shoes on his sockless feet. Where his wife was all cool elegance and understated sex appeal, he radiated roguish bad-boy charm and heated sexuality. He was the kind of man women lost their heads over, and Willow could easily believe every scandalous word ever written about him in the tabloids.

"Zeke Blackstone," he said, offering his hand as if he were just like plain folks. "Sit down, please." He motioned them toward the sofa, perching himself on the arm of one of the oversize chairs. "Jack Shannon left me a rather cryptic message on my answering machine yesterday about making sure I talked to you when you called," he said. "But when I called him back, he wouldn't tell me what it was about. Said it would be better if I was surprised. Writers," he said with good-natured disgust. "Always so dramatic."

He popped up from his perch as his wife came back into the room, reaching out to take the tray she carried and place it on the coffee table. "All I know is that this has something to do with a young woman who used to live at the Bachelor Arms back in '70." He handed them each a glass of chilled white wine, took one for himself, and sat down next to his wife. "How can I help you?" he asked.

Willow hesitated and glanced at Ariel Cameron.

"You can ask him about old girlfriends in front of me," Ariel said with a smile. "I'm shockproof."

"Well . . ." The best way, Willow had found, was just to ask. Hemming and hawing wouldn't make it easier for any of them. "I was wondering if you might be my father."

Ariel Cameron might have been shockproof but her husband wasn't. He nearly spilled his wine all over himself. His wife reached out and rescued it, leaning forward to place it on the table. "Could you elaborate on that statement?" she asked calmly.

ZEKE BLACKSTONE sat staring down at the pictures Willow had handed him. "I never dated your mother," he said. "And that's God's honest truth. If it would put your mind at ease, I'd be happy to take a blood test."

"No, that would be—"

"Maybe at a later date," Steve interrupted before Willow could let the other man off the hook completely.

Willow shot him a chastising look out of the corner of her eye; to her way of thinking, the very fact that

Zeke Blackstone had offered to take a blood test indicated the truth of what he'd said.

"Do you recall anything about Donna Ryan?" Steve asked. "Who she might have dated, that sort of thing?"

"She was Eric's girlfriend."

Steve and Willow looked at each other. "Eric's, not Ethan's?" Steve said, just to be sure.

"Actually..." He frowned, thinking, then shrugged. "That whole situation was a little weird. She dated Ethan a couple of times right after she moved into the BA, maybe even three or four times. And then she and Eric got involved. Pretty seriously, I thought."

"Do you know if they were intimate?"

"I thought so at the time but..." He shrugged. "Who really knows what goes on between two people? Later, after Eric died, I wondered about it."

"Why was that?"

"Ethan was annoyed when she started dating Eric. They almost got into a knock-down-drag-out over it. The two guys, I mean. Apparently, Ethan thought that, since he'd been the one who had brought her to the BA, as it were, she should be his exclusive property. He wasn't happy about sharing."

"Were they?" Steve asked, elaborating when Zeke looked at him. "Sharing?"

"I don't know." He glanced at Willow, his gaze apologetic. "Maybe. It was a pretty volatile situation. And then, after Eric committed suicide, she seemed to turn to Ethan for comfort. It was like she felt guilty and Ethan was the only one who would understand. Now, you've got to take into account that I was pretty much in a blue funk myself at the time—that night changed things for everyone in 1-G—but I seem to remember them talking a lot about the lady in the mirror and how it had affected their lives and what her appearance really meant. They were very intense about it. It gave me the creeps."

"Don't tell me," Steve said dryly. "They'd both thought they'd seen her, right?"

"Oh, yeah," Zeke said easily. "Ethan did at least twice that I know of. The first time was just before he got the part on 'As Time Goes By.' The second was the night Eric died. He was—maybe still is for all I know—completely convinced that the legend is true."

Steve snorted. "No wonder our political system is going down the toilet."

Zeke laughed. "It wasn't only Ethan," he said. "Apparently, lots of people have seen her over the years. It's one of those things I'd normally discount as a product of the overactive imaginations of people who should know better, but Jack Shannon swears he and his wife saw her, too."

"Yes, he did." Steve grinned. "And that sweet-faced wife of his nearly took my head off for me when I doubted him."

Zeke laughed. "That sweet face fools a lot of people," he said. "Little Faith is a tiger where Jack is concerned."

"Have you seen the woman in the mirror?" Willow asked.

Zeke shook his head. "Not that I recall."

"I have," Ariel said.

Her husband turned to look at her. "You have? When?"

She gave him an intimate, wifely smile. "That first time we went back there together after we started 'dating' again."

"Why didn't you say anything before now?"

"It was just a fleeting glance, and I wasn't really sure I'd seen anything, so I kind of forgot about it. Hearing you talk about it now reminded me of it."

"Do you think it changed your life?" Willow asked.

Ariel shrugged. "Zeke and I are back together. If you'd asked me if I thought that would ever have happened before that day in the apartment when I saw her, I'd've said there wasn't a chance in a million. And yet—"she smiled at her husband "—here we are, happier than we've ever been."

"And you think that's due to some ghost in a mirror?" Steve scoffed.

"I don't know. Maybe. There's something almost..." Ariel waved her hand gracefully "...otherworldly about that apartment. It affects people in strange ways."

"Jack is convinced something in it brought us all back to the Bachelor Arms . . . to the scene of the crime, as it were," Zeke said. "Him first, so he could come to terms with his brother's suicide, and then me and Ariel." He pursed his lips, giving them a look from under his brows. "And now you. It makes a person wonder."

"IT MAKES A PERSON WONDER about other people's sanity," Steve groused, as he paid the vendor for their ice cream. They'd stopped for dinner at a chi chi little outdoor café with a view of the ocean. Afterward, instead of lingering over coffee and dessert, they opted for ice-cream cones and a walk on the beach. "How grown people can believe that kind of mystical mumbo-jumbo nonsense is beyond me."

Willow laughed at him. "What was it Jack Shannon said the other night? 'There are more things in heaven and earth than are dreamt of'? Or something like that." She tilted her head, licking at her ice cream where it threatened to drip down over her thumb. "Don't you believe there's more to this world than things we can hear and see and touch?"

"No," Steve said blunty, watching her little pink tongue dart in and out, swirling around the frozen confection, lapping it up before the melting rivulets of ice cream dripped over her fingers. He knew she wasn't being intentionally provocative but . . . damn, she was turning him on! He passed a quick, furtive hand over the front of his jeans, giving them a quick tug to ease the pressure. "The real world is more than enough for me to deal with," he said in a strangled voice.

"Who's to say what's real and what isn't?" Willow asked, her attention focused on her melting Mocha Fudge. "Philosophers have been arguing that question for centur— Oh, your ice cream!" she exclaimed, as his double scoop of Strawberry Delight, cone and all, plopped into the sand at their feet. "Well, that's all right," she said soothingly, as if he were about five years old, "you can have some of mi—" She stopped, caught by the look in his blue eyes. It took her a moment to catch her breath. "You aren't the least bit interested in sharing my ice cream, are you?"

"Sure I am." He reached out and caught her wrist in his, holding it still while the ice cream melted. Then, his hot-eyed gaze holding hers, he brought her hand to his mouth and slowly, oh-so-slowly, licked the cool, sticky confection from her fingers.

Willow gasped and dropped her cone.

"Do you want another one?" Steve murmured, already knowing what her answer would be.

Speechless, Willow shook her head.

"Then let's go home." He grinned wickedly. "But let's get a quart of this stuff to take with us." He sucked her index finger into his mouth and drew it out slowly. "It tastes real good on you."

THE MESSAGE LIGHT was blinking on Steve's answering machine when they got back to his house, a silent, insistent beacon that immediately broke the sensual mood. Steve put the ice cream in the freezer and pushed the Play button.

"I finally tracked down that box of stuff," Jack Shannon said. "Amberson has it. He removed it from 1-G while Faith and I were moving and put it back in the basement at Bachelor Arms. Said that's where it belongs, if you can believe it." Willow could almost see the unbelieving lift of his eyebrow. "I'm going over to get it tomorrow morning. You can meet me there around ten and pick it up then, or wait and come by the apartment later in the week. Faith said she'd be happy to have you for dinner Wednesday or Thursday. It's up to you."

Willow shivered with sudden anticipation, like a greyhound before a race. Steve reached out and put his arm around her. "We'll pick it up tomorrow morning," he told her, giving her shoulders a little squeeze.

"Marty here," the next voice said. "You were right about that Ryan case. It was a hit-and-run. Never did catch the perp, so the case is still open. Call me at the station tomorrow, buddy. I'd be real interested to hear why *you're* so interested in it."

"Well," Willow said softly. "I guess that pretty much settles it."

"No," Steve said thoughtfully. "No, I don't think it does." He put a hand to his stomach, unconsciously rubbing at the spot where his gut spoke to him. "There's something not right about this case," he said. "There's something more involved than just whether or not Ethan Roberts is trying to keep the world from finding out you might be his daughter."

"What do you mean?"

"The scandal that might result from that isn't enough to justify what happened yesterday. If you took it to the papers, it'd be a big splashy headline for about two days and then disappear. Roberts' political career would hardly feel the ripples. He's afraid of something else."

"That we'll find out he murdered my mother."

"Yeah, that's part of it. But there's more." He rubbed at his stomach again, just below the breastbone where his instincts lived. "I can feel it."

12

"DO YOU THINK this will work?" Willow said as Steve
pushed open the wrought-iron courtyard gate to the
Bachelor Arms and ushered her in ahead of him.

"We won't know until we try," he said. "Roberts was
pretty cool and cagey on the phone, as if he had no idea
and less interest in my theories about what happened
to your mother." He grinned evilly. "I could hear him
sweating."

They crossed the quiet courtyard, the heels of Willow's red leather sling-backs clicking softly against the
pebbled concrete surface, sounding unnaturally loud
in the somnolent silence. The gracious old building
seemed to be napping in the midmorning sun, like an
elderly lady who'd fallen asleep on the porch while she
waited for someone to come.

The temperature seemed to drop ten degrees as they
pushed open the door into the downstairs corridor. The
silence intensified, growing suddenly...eerie. Willow
shivered and moved closer to Steve, slipping her hand
through the crook of his arm. The door to apartment
1-G stood partially open, offering them entrance in
mute invitation. They hesitated at the threshold, each
mentally preparing themselves for whatever was to
come.

Steve looked down at the woman by his side. "You don't have to do this. I'd rather you didn't."

Willow straightened her spine. "I have to," she declared, and let go of his arm to walk through the door on her own.

The apartment was empty, the box of old memories and secrets nowhere in sight. "I guess Jack and Amberson must still be down in the basement looking for it," Steve said.

Willow walked to the mirror. "It's hard to imagine that so many people have been affected by this, isn't it?" She reached out, touching the intricate pewter scrolls and roses that adorned the frame. "It's just an old mirror."

"It's more than a mirror," said a voice behind her.

She whirled around.

Ethan Roberts stood in the open doorway of one of the bedrooms. He was dressed in a custom-tailored, conservative blue suit, a white shirt and a striped red tie. He was the epitome of a successful politician: conservative, well dressed, urbane and blandly agreeble.

Except for the gun in his hand.

"It's a looking glass into the future," he said pleasantly, as if he were making an inconsequential comment at a cocktail party. "If you stare at it long enough you'll see your whole life reflected it in. If the lady wants you to," he added. "She's always been very good to me."

"I thought you said you'd never seen her," Steve challenged, trying to draw Ethan's attention away from Willow.

"I lied," Roberts admitted, without taking his eyes off of Willow or the mirror. "It wouldn't be prudent for a man in my position to admit that he believes in ghosts, now would it? The voters wouldn't like it. Don't move, Hart," he ordered, his voice going steely. "I wouldn't want to have to shoot you. Or Ms. Ryan."

"What are you planning to do with us?" Steve asked, as if it were a minor point of curiosity.

"I've arranged a little accident," he said. "Not another hit-and-run. That might be a bit too obvious. A fire this time, I think. It will be very tragic. Two young lovers burned to death in a remote house out in Laurel Canyon because their smoke detectors needed new batteries."

"There are too many people who know this time, Roberts. Jack Shannon and Amberson are in the basement right now. They know we're meeting you here. If we show up dead, they'll know it was you."

"They might suspect," Ethan agreed. "But they'll never know. Neither one of them will ever be able to say they actually saw me here, or that they saw you. No, I didn't kill them," he said, seeing the horrified look on Willow's face. "I locked them in the basement when they went down to look for that box. This time of day, with all the tenants at work, it'll be hours before someone lets them out. As far as they'll know, none of us ever showed up at all. It'll look like the two of you delayed your departure for a little morning quickie and burned up more than the sheets."

"You won't get away with it."

"I'll get away with it," Roberts said, with the confidence of a spoiled child who's always gotten his way. "I always have before. Murder is actually very easy, you know. If you take the right precautions and do it yourself so there's never anyone else involved who can betray you, it's very simple. No one ever finds out."

"We found out," Steve said. "We know you killed your ex-wife."

"Suicide from a drug overdose," Ethan said dismissively. "She was distraught about losing the boys. Everyone agreed on that, even the police."

"And my mother," Willow said. "You killed her, too. Why?"

Roberts' face twisted suddenly, becoming ugly. "Because she was a lying slut who betrayed me with Eric Shannon. *I* was the one who discovered her. *I* was the one who brought her to the Bachelor Arms. She was supposed to be *mine*."

"And she didn't want anything to do with you, did she, Roberts?" Steve taunted. "She only went out with you because the studio pressured her to. And then she started dating Eric Shannon and refused to go out with you anymore."

"She didn't understand what I could give her. What we could be together. I had to make her understand."

"How? How did you make her understand?"

"I followed her and Eric up to her apartment the night of the party. Eric had just had a fight with his brother about a script they'd sold to Regal Productions and he wanted her to comfort him. I waited outside her bedroom door, listening to them making love like animals, and then later, when she was asleep and Eric went out on the balcony for a cigarette, I pushed him over," he said as calmly as if he'd just admitted to nothing more heinous than taking out the trash. "Then I went back downstairs to the party in 1-G. When Donna came down later and asked where Eric was, somebody told her they thought he'd gone out for more beer. An idea I planted," he said proudly. "It was a couple of hours before anybody found the body. Zeke stumbled over him when he was chasing Ariel after she found him in bed with another woman, did he tell you that?"

"He told us that Donna turned to you after Eric's death. Did you plan that, too?"

"I understood her," he said. "I sympathized. I even forgave her for what she did with Eric, until she told me she was pregnant with his bastard."

Willow gasped.

"Yes, Eric Shannon is your father, Ms. Ryan. Does it comfort you to know that?"

"Yes," she breathed. "Yes, it comforts me a great deal."

"You have no more taste than she did," he said dismissively.

"Why did you wait over a year to kill her?" Steve asked. "Why not do it when you found out she was pregnant?"

"Because she ran," Ethan said. "And I didn't know where she'd gone. She came back later, saying she was sorry and that she wanted to take up where we'd left off. But she was lying. She suspected me of killing Eric and she was trying to find the proof. There was no proof and I told her so. She threatened to go to the police with her suspicions. I couldn't let that happen. I'd been signed to play the heroic lead in a Western, and that kind of publicity—even though she couldn't have proven anything—could have killed it."

"So you killed her instead. Just like that."

"Yes. As I said, murder's easy. I disguised myself, stole a car out of a parking lot and ran her down. I parked the car in the street about six blocks from there and walked away."

"Don't you feel any remorse?" Willow said, unable to grasp the enormity of it. He'd murdered three people without blinking an eye. *Three people*—that they knew of. "How do you sleep at night?"

"Quite soundly, actually."

"He's a classic psychopath," Steve said. "No conscience. No morals. No soul. Okay, Marty," he said, raising his voice a bit as if he were talking to someone outside the room. "I think we've got enough."

Ethan looked toward Steve. "I thought you were more of a professional than to try that old gag," he sneered.

Slowly, keeping his hands in plain sight, Steve pulled down the collar of his sport shirt and showed him the wires.

Ethan Roberts' face turned purple with rage. *"No!"* he screamed, firing the gun at Steve as he rushed him.

Steve took the shot in the chest and kept coming. He tackled Roberts, knocking him back against the wall. The gun flew out of Roberts' hand, clattering against the wooden floor, and went whirling away, round and round like a child's deadly top.

"Pick it up," Steve ordered, but Willow was already bending down, scrambling after it.

"You can't do this to me," Roberts stormed, as Steve kept him pressed up against the wall with a forearm across his throat, waiting for the police backup who were already flooding into the room. "This is illegal. I'm a representative in the California State Legislature. I demand—" He stopped suddenly, his whole body going stiff, and stared over Steve's shoulder with a look of horror on his face.

Steve twisted his head around, looking over his shoulder to see what the other man was staring at. The shining surface of the pewter-framed mirror reflected their images back at him.

"You see her, don't you?" Steve taunted, turning back to face Roberts. "The lady in the mirror is staring at you, isn't she? Well—" he grinned evilly, pressing his forearm harder against Roberts' throat "—congratulations. Your worst nightmare is about to come true."

"I THOUGHT THOSE bulletproof vests were supposed to protect you from bullets," Willow said, as she stood in the middle of apartment 1-G and gently probed the ugly bruise forming just below and a little to the left of where Steve's heart beat in his chest. She had insisted on inspecting his injury immediately, rudely pushing away the policeman who was busy relieving him of both vest and wires. "This looks as if someone hit you with a baseball bat."

She glared at the policeman as if it were his fault. "Don't you have bulletproof vests that offer any better protection than this?" she demanded.

"No, ma'am," he said, unperturbed by her attack. "That's the top of the line. I'll need the one you have on, too, ma'am."

Willow shrugged out of her red jacket and the flowered print vest beneath, revealing the police-issue bulletproof vest she wore under that. She turned her back, letting the policeman slip it down over the white silk sleeves of her blouse.

The policeman thanked her politely, then turned and left the room, following his fellow officers.

Willow had already turned her attention back to Steve. "Does it feel like your rib is broken?" she asked anxiously.

"Only when you poke at it like that," he said, wincing as he batted her fingers away.

She looked up, her eyes stricken. "Oh, God, I'm sorry." She curled her hands into fists to keep from touching him. "I didn't mean to hurt you. I'm sorry, I—"

"Willow." He dropped his shirt and took her fists in his hands. "Willow, it's all right. It's over."

"It's over." She closed her eyes for a minute, trying to gather her control. "Yes, it's over," she said, giving up the battle as she leaned into him and touched her forehead to his chest. He wrapped his arms around her and cradled her close.

They stood like that for a few long moments, just holding each other, glad to be alive. And whole. And together.

She lifted her head then, and smiled up into his face. "I love you," she said softly. "I just thought you should know."

He shook his head. "Not yet," he said. "Wait until you've had time to come down from this."

She narrowed her eyes indignantly. "Are you suggesting that I don't know what I'm saying? That this is some sort of adrenaline-induced emotion?"

"Something like that," Steve said, amused by her vehemence.

"Well, of all the arrogant . . . If you weren't already bruised, I swear, Steve Hart, I'd punch you so hard you'd feel it into next week." She shook her head as if she couldn't believe what he'd said. "It's only because you've been wounded that I'm cutting you some slack this time. I won't be so lenient again." She slid her arms up around his neck. "I love you, Steve Hart," she said, staring up into his eyes as she repeated the words. "And I will always love you, you overgrown Boy Scout, so get used to it."

"Willow, I . . ."

She smiled, pleased, for once, to have rendered him speechless. "Just shut up and kiss me," she ordered and pulled his head down to hers.

"Ahem!" said a voice from behind them. "Am I interrupting something?"

"Yes," Steve said, and placed one last lingering kiss on Willow's lips before turning his head to see who it was. Jack Shannon stood in the hallway leading to the front door of apartment 1-G with a cardboard box in his arms.

"I thought you might want to look at this right away," he said, coming into the room with it. "There's a lot of interesting stuff in here." He bent over, putting it down on the floor, and then straightened and held his hand out to Steve. "I can't thank you enough," he said. "Finding out that Eric didn't commit suicide is like having a weight lifted off my chest that I didn't even know was there."

"Thank Willow," Steve said as he shook the other man's hand. "She's the one who insisted she had to know what happened."

"I'd like to kiss her instead, if I may," he said, suiting his actions to his words. "Welcome to the family, Willow," he said as he pressed his lips against her cheek.

Willow threw her arms around him and held tight for a long moment. "Thank you." She pulled back and smiled a little, teasingly, through her happy tears. "Uncle Jack," she said.

Jack groaned. "That sounds just a bit weird coming from a woman who's the same age as my wife," he said, and then smiled. "But I guess I could get used to it."

"You'd better," Steve said, "because she'll use it every chance she gets. The woman has a smart mouth on her."

Jack and Willow exchanged another quick hug. "We'll expect you both for dinner next Wednesday," he said, and left them alone with the box and the mirror.

They knelt down on the floor, the cardboard box between them.

"I'm shaking," Willow admitted. "You do it."

Steve reached into the box and pulled out the treasures that had been hidden for twenty-five years. There were more pictures. And cards from Donna to Eric. And a journal.

Donna told me today that she's going to have my baby, Eric had written. *It makes everything so perfect.*

And there it was, the dream Willow thought she had lost. The father who had loved her mother and was separated from her and their unborn baby through no fault of his own.

"Oh, Steve," she said, tears in her eyes and in her voice. "Steve, I—" She stopped suddenly, mesmerized by what she saw in the mirror behind him.

Seeing the look on her face, he turned toward the mirror, too.

"Do you see her?" she whispered.

Steve blinked, trying to clear his vision. "I . . . my God, yes," he admitted. "I see her."

They sat there for a moment, on their knees with the box between them, watching the lady in the long pale dress. She looked at them consideringly for a moment, and then she nodded and smiled gently, and disappeared.

Willow and Steve turned to look at each other, both of them a little awed by the magic of what had just happened.

"I guess that means your greatest dream has come true," Steve said, touching the box that sat on the floor between them.

"Yes, it has." Willow reached out and covered his hand with hers. "But it's more than just what's in this box."

"It is?"

"You know it is." Willow pushed the box out of the way and moved across the small space that separated them. "You saw her, too."

"Yeah, well . . ." He shrugged.

"Don't you dare try to back out of it now, tough guy," she warned, reaching up to put her hands on either side of his face so he couldn't look away. "You already admitted it."

He put his hands on her waist and looked down at her. "How 'bout if I just plead the Fifth?"

"Too late. We both saw her. *Together.*"

"Meaning?" he teased, knowing full well what she was getting at.

"Meaning we're about to attain *our* greatest dream." She tilted her head, looking up at him from under her lashes, her lips a teasing, tempting millimeter away from his as she asked the question. "Aren't we?"

"You better believe it, sweetheart," he said with his Bogie imitation, and bent his head to kiss her.

Epilogue

THE WHISPERS OF SCANDAL were first heard on a local afternoon newscast the day Ethan Roberts was arrested. By that evening, the Los Angeles press had printed several versions of the story, among them a front page article in the *L.A. Times* under Jack Shannon's by line which detailed the nefarious career of Ethan Roberts. By the next morning the tale of the murderous Senate hopeful was in every newspaper and every tabloid; it was being discussed on every talk show on television; and hotly debated in car pools and around office water coolers everywhere.

An army of reporters and TV camera crews rushed to camp outside the gate of the Roberts' Pacific Palisades estate and 'Hard Copy' had sent a reporter to Steve's Laurel Canyon home in an effort to track down the detective who had broken the story.

But Willow and Steve had disappeared.

"I GUESS HIS GREATEST nightmare really has come true," Willow said as CNN Headline News finished a segment on Ethan Roberts' arraignment for murder at the Los Angeles County courthouse.

"Yeah." Steve's voice was rich with satisfaction. "Everybody in the world knows what a no-good, murdering sleaze he is."

"Still . . ." Willow sat down on the edge of the huge round hotel bed. "I can't help but feel sorry for his family. That sweet little girl of his has got to be hurting and confused right now."

"That sweet little girl will be a lot better off in the long run without Ethan Roberts in her life," Steve said, reaching over to take the remote control out of Willow's hand.

"Hey," she objected as the television screen went black. "The stock market report is next."

"Wall Street will still be there tomorrow," he said, setting the remote out of her reach on the dresser.

She gave him a narrowed look. "I want to watch it now," she insisted, just to see what he would say.

"And I want to make love to my wife. Now."

Willow nearly melted as heat sizzled through her. *Wife.* It was such a lovely word. A sexy word. A powerful word. She'd been hearing it for two full days, ever since the quickie ceremony in the Las Vegas wedding chapel; she should be used to it by now. But every time he said it, in that low, suggestive, possessive tone of voice, her insides turned into molten lava and her brains turned to mush. She was beginning to suspect it would always be that way.

"No objections?" Steve asked, giving her a slow, knowing grin as he reached up to loosen his tie.

Willow rallied to the challenge implicit in his eyes. "No," she said, her hand going to the top button on her fitted black evening jacket. "No objections." She lowered her head, giving him a provocative look from under her lashes. "It'll be on again in half an hour."

His grin widened appreciatively. "Is that a dare, Mrs. Hart?"

Willow unfastened the last button of her jacket. "What do you think, Mr. Hart?" she purred and squeezed her forearms together slightly, so that her breasts mounded above the square-cut décolletage of her dress.

It was Steve's turn to melt a little. "I think it's going to take a lot longer than half an hour," he growled, and dropped his tie to the floor.

They began a slow, teasing striptease for each other.

He peeled off his shirt, slowly, like a Chippendale dancer.

She removed her jacket, slowly, rolling her shoulders like a Las Vegas show girl.

He unbuckled his belt and released the top button on his slacks, letting them sag open over his flat, washboard abdomen.

She unzipped her dress, leaning forward so that the bodice dropped to her waist and pooled in her lap.

He sat down on the tacky zebra-striped chair behind him and yanked off his shoes and socks.

She leaned over and reached for the black satin ankle strap of her high-heeled shoe.

"Leave them on," he growled, low.

Willow looked up, her body still bent, her hair swinging down over her cheek. "My shoes?" she asked, just to be sure.

"I've had this persistent fantasy about you and those shoes." He stood, barefoot, and yanked the zipper of his slacks the rest of the way down. "About making love to you while you were wearing them." He let the slacks drop to the floor and calmly, slowly and very purposefully shed his briefs. "And nothing else."

Willow licked her lips in excitement and anticipation, her eyes widening as he crossed the room toward her, gloriously naked and magnificently aroused.

He put his hands on her shoulders, pushing her flat against the quilted red satin bedspread, then curled his hands into the stretchy fabric of the dress bunched around her waist. In one quick move, he pulled it down over her hips and legs, and tossed it on the floor. She lay there, staring up at him, breathless with desire, wearing only black satin panties, seamed thigh-high stockings and her high-heeled shoes.

It was Steve's turn to lick his lips. "This is better than the fantasy," he murmured, reaching out to peel the panties off. "Much better."

They stared at each other for a long breathless second: Willow lying on her back on the bed, provocative, alluring and female, powerful in willing surrender; Steve looming over her, all raw male passion and masculine aggression, gentle in mastery. They were hot eyed and wanting, both of them trembling with desire and anticipation, hearts pounding, pulses racing, aching with love.

The playfulness faded from their eyes as they stared at each other. The teasing game was over as quickly as it had begun.

Steve lowered himself on top of her, gently, his chest to her breasts, his hips between her thighs, holding himself up on his elbows as he cupped her face in his hands.

"I love you," he murmured, looking deeply into her eyes as he said it.

Willow wrapped herself around him. "I love you, too, tough guy."

* * * * *

COMING UP IN BACHELOR ARMS

Prosecutor Clint McCreary's greatest fear is that he'll lose the armor of cynicism he's spent years developing. While searching for his runaway teenage sister, he moves into Bachelor Arms and his fears start to come true. First Clint, a disbeliever in anything unusual, sees the resident ghost. And then he meets Jessie Gale, the one woman who could break through his shell and hurt him badly. To top it all off, he sees a real-life flesh-and-blood woman who resembles the Bachelor Arms ghost....

Find out the conclusion to the legend in Judith Arnold's captivating:
#561 THE LADY IN THE MIRROR (November 1995)
#565 TIMELESS LOVE (December 1995)
Believe the Legend...

BACHELOR ARMS SURVEY

TALES OF TRANSFORMATION!
From Confirmed Bachelors to Super Suitors!

What is the best way to land a bachelor?

1. Home Cooking—the way to every man's heart
2. Jealousy—set loose the green-eyed monster
3. Temptation—dress for success
4. Game Playing—ignore him, feign indifference
5. Role Reversal—romance *him* for a change
6. Be Frugal—move in together to save money; once you've got him, don't let go

We want to hear from you, so please send in your responses to:

> In the U.S.: BACHELOR ARMS,
> P.O. Box 9076, Buffalo, NY 14269-9076
>
> In Canada: BACHELOR ARMS,
> P.O. Box 637, Ft. Erie, ON L2A 5X3

Name: _____

Address:_____ City:_____

State/Prov.:. _____ Zip/Postal Code:_____

Please note that all entries become the property of Harlequin and we may publish them in any publication, with credit at our discretion.

OFFICIAL RULES

PRIZE SURPRISE SWEEPSTAKES 3448

NO PURCHASE OR OBLIGATION NECESSARY

Three Harlequin Reader Service 1995 shipments will contain respectively, coupons for entry into three different prize drawings, one for a Panasonic 31" wide-screen TV, another for a 5-piece Wedgwood china service for eight and the third for a Sharp ViewCam camcorder. To enter any drawing using an Entry Coupon, simply complete and mail according to directions.

There is no obligation to continue using the Reader Service to enter and be eligible for any prize drawing. You may also enter any drawing by hand printing the words "Prize Surprise," your name and address on a 3"x5" card and the name of the prize you wish that entry to be considered for (i.e., Panasonic wide-screen TV, Wedgwood china or Sharp ViewCam). Send your 3"x5" entries via first-class mail (limit: one per envelope) to: Prize Surprise Sweepstakes 3448, c/o the prize you wish that entry to be considered for, P.O. Box 1315, Buffalo, NY 14269-1315, USA or P.O. Box 610, Fort Erie, Ontario L2A 5X3, Canada.

To be eligible for the Panasonic wide-screen TV, entries must be received by 6/30/95; for the Wedgwood china, 8/30/95; and for the Sharp ViewCam, 10/30/95.

Winners will be determined in random drawings conducted under the supervision of D.L. Blair, Inc., an independent judging organization whose decisions are final, from among all eligible entries received for that drawing. Approximate prize values are as follows: Panasonic wide-screen TV ($1,800); Wedgwood china ($840) and Sharp ViewCam ($2,000). Sweepstakes open to residents of the U.S. (except Puerto Rico) and Canada, 18 years of age or older. Employees and immediate family members of Harlequin Enterprises, Ltd., D.L. Blair, Inc., their affiliates, subsidiaries and all other agencies, entities and persons connected with the use, marketing or conduct of this sweepstakes are not eligible. Odds of winning a prize are dependent upon the number of eligible entries received for that drawing. Prize drawing and winner notification for each drawing will occur no later than 15 days after deadline for entry eligibility for that drawing. Limit: one prize to an individual, family or organization. All applicable laws and regulations apply. Sweepstakes offer void wherever prohibited by law. Any litigation within the province of Quebec respecting the conduct and awarding of the prizes in this sweepstakes must be submitted to the Regies des loteries et Courses du Quebec. In order to win a prize, residents of Canada will be required to correctly answer a time-limited arithmetical skill-testing question. Value of prizes are in U.S. currency.

Winners will be obligated to sign and return an Affidavit of Eligibility within 30 days of notification. In the event of noncompliance within this time period, prize may not be awarded. If any prize or prize notification is returned as undeliverable, that prize will not be awarded. By acceptance of a prize, winner consents to use of his/her name, photograph or other likeness for purposes of advertising, trade and promotion on behalf of Harlequin Enterprises, Ltd., without further compensation, unless prohibited by law.

For the names of prizewinners (available after 12/31/95), send a self-addressed, stamped envelope to: Prize Surprise Sweepstakes 3448 Winners, P.O. Box 4200, Blair, NE 68009.

RPZ KAL